PAINTED OXEN

A NOVEL

PAINTED OXEN

A NOVEL

THOMAS LLOYD QUALLS

Homebound Publications
Ensuring the Mainstream Isn't the Only Stream

HOMEBOUND PUBLICATIONS
Ensuring the Mainstream Isn't the Only Stream | *Since* 2011
WWW.HOMEBOUNDPUBLICATIONS.COM

Quantity sales. Special discounts are available on quantity purchases by corporations, associations, bookstores and others. For details, contact the publisher at the address below or visit wholesalers such as Ingram or Baker & Taylor. Homebound Publications, P.O. 1442, Pawcatuck, Connecticut 06379.

Published in 2019 by Homebound Publications
Cover & Interior Designed by Leslie M. Browning
Interior Photo (Title Page) © by Sangay Lama
Interior Photo (Taj Mahal) © by Annie Spratt
Interior Photo (Varanasi at Sunrise) © by Stellalevi | iStock.com
Interior Map © by Tonello Photography | Shutterstock.com
Cover Photo © by Federico Gutierrez
ISBN 978-1-947003-36-1
First Edition Trade Paperback

10 9 8 7 6 5 4 3 2 1

Homebound Publications is committed to ecological stewardship. We greatly value the natural environment and invest in environmental conservation. Our books are printed on paper with chain of custody certification from the Forest Stewardship Council, Sustainable Forestry Initiative, and the Program for the Endorsement of Forest Certification.

THIS BOOK IS DEDICATED TO
KYRA LILY
AND TO THE DREAMER IN EACH OF YOU.

~

NEPAL
KATMANDU
BHUTAN
THIMPHU
BANGLADESH
DHAKA
Patna
Gange
DELHI
Agra
Kanpur
Benares/
Varanasi
Calcutta
Bhopal
Nagpur
INDIA
Hyderabad
Surat
Bombay/
Mumbai
Madras/
Bangalore
Mangalore
Cochin/
Kochi

INVITO

THIS IS A DIFFERENT KIND OF BOOK. One that not only invites you to come along for its journey, but to participate in its story. There are places in these pages you have forgotten exist. It is time to remember.

This is the story of two men, one young and one old, on separate pilgrimages that are equal parts internal and external. The old man, a Tibetan monk, is searching for a sacred hidden valley known to bring enlightenment to those who enter it. The young man is a modern-day backpacker who has traveled to India in the age-old tradition of seeking higher truths about himself and the world. The story moves back and forth between these two characters and weaves together a tale of their parallel journeys that are centuries apart, but may be more connected than they appear.

There are four winds, four elements, and four seasons. In this spirit, the novel is arranged in sets of four. Two of the four parts are the stories of the old man and the young man, titled *Scylla* and *Charybdis*, respectively, after the dual perils faced by Homer's Odysseus.

The third part is a series of dreams. Presented as fragments of interrelated stories involving a goddess with red hair, an alchemist, a pair of lions, and the god Vishnu, these visually lush vignettes act as connective tissue for the two main stories. Because we must smuggle our dreams into the waking world, these chapters are titled *Praeda*, which means *stolen goods*. The main character in the dream world is the mysterious red-haired woman who holds ancient secrets and who acts as a guide of sorts for the dreamer.

The tales of the two pilgrims, together with the dream stories, each make up a trinity of vignettes, and each of these trinities carries a theme, introduced to the reader by a character from the 22 major arcana of the Tarot—a deck of cards that dates back to at least the 15th Century—thus creating the fourth dimension and squaring the set. One of these 22 cards is the Fool. Like our two protagonists, the Fool must leave the safety of his home in the Sacred Mountain in order to embark upon the journey of Life. Likewise, each Tarot card represents a stage in life that we must pass through on our journey back to the Sacred Mountain.

Each realm also uses its own voice. A voice is an important thing to have, whether or not you are a character in a novel. The old man's story is told in third person, because a Tibetan Buddhist would never tell his own story. The young man's story is told in first person, because telling their own stories is exactly what backpackers do. Finally, the dream world thread is told in second person, because it takes place between the other two worlds. And because, after all, you are the dreamer.

As I mentioned, this is a different kind of book. If you accept its invitation, you must understand that—like the characters in these pages—you will find yourself transformed by its journey's end.

THE STORY

PRAEDA

A CANDLE BURNS IN THE DARKNESS of the small room, melting wax abandoning its safe purchase and falling down the bending sides of what once was a knowable and dependable form. You stand at a rough workbench, your labors exposed only through the faint glow of its flickering revelations. Your fingers are stained and scorched, your sleeves pushed up beyond your elbows. Stones and flints, shavings and sparkling fragments lay scattered before you. There are containers of clear and dark liquids, a measuring device, and a notebook open to a page of scribbles and drawings.

Your quest is an ancient one. To change the nature of matter, to harness the power of the elements in the dance of creation, to create perfection from imperfection, to steal fire from the gods.

Gold is valued not only for its luminous appearance but also because of its transitional nature, which we do not fully understand. It is both trivalent and univalent. In other words, it walks in many worlds, effortlessly crossing barriers. It represents transformation, eternity, perfection. One who knows the secrets of gold holds the keys to the human heart. One who masters the alchemy of gold, unlocks the mysteries of the universe.

You bend over the table, the mandala of colors before you, your hands holding the elements, your mind focused on harmonics, your ears trained to the language of the stars, your spirit tuned to the oneness of all things. Time sputters and slows, bending to match your rhythm.

THE FOOL

The first and unnumbered of the major arcana is the Fool. He is leaving the spiritual mountain and, with naive purity, is about to step off a cliff and embark upon an epic adventure, the Fool's Journey, traveling through the gates of Divine Wisdom. This is so, even though the purpose of the Fool's Journey is to find the sacred mountain from which he came. He must leave so he can return.

–THE BOOK OF MYSTERIES

SCYLLA

THE MONK AWAKES FROM A DREAM to the sound of rain. The dream is one he has had before. In it he is not dressed in his traditional robes, but in a manner he does not recognize. He is a much younger man on a long journey far from home, and he is lost. The young man set out on his adventure with noble intentions, to discover higher truths about himself and the universe. Though now, cut loose from all that is familiar, he has begun to wander without purpose. And he is near despair.

The young wanderer is looking for an answer to a question he has not yet asked. While he travels, he meets many people, each of whom has wisdom to share. But because the young man is looking for a grand treasure, he cannot see the small gifts he finds along the way. As such, he does not yet understand the true nature of the universe.

At one time or another we are all called to leave the safety of our homes, the certainty of what we know, the illusions of who we are. Not everyone will heed this call, of course. And those who do will risk losing themselves completely. But if we choose to ignore the invitation, we risk never knowing who we might have become. We risk dying without knowing what it is to live.

The monk, too, has left his home. Though he travels not from city to city, but through far more inhospitable territory, over mountains, across valleys, beside river gorges, and along sheer cliffs. He wears little more than his saffron robes. What land and stream cannot provide for him in order to survive, he carries on his back. The sound he hears as he awakes in his shelter—nothing more than a woolen robe stretched between low-lying tree limbs—signals the eighth straight day of torrential rains. At least the rain keeps at bay the snakes and large predators.

He seeks the hidden heart of the world. This journey is his life's work, and he must be disciplined. Unlike the younger man in his dream, the monk must resist the urge to wander. He must not allow himself to become lost. And he must not succumb to the allure of despair. He must protect the spark of truth that lives inside him.

Prometheus stole fire from the gods. We are the heirs of that divine spark. Used wisely, the spark fuels one's journey and lights the way. Treated carelessly, the spark consumes its owner and everything in its path.

*   *   *   *

Long ago, when he, too, was a young man, his master explained that there are three worlds in which we live. There is the waking world, the spirit world, and the dream world. The waking world is that which we believe is real, and yet it is mostly illusion. Because we cannot see it, the spirit world is the one we believe is fantasy, and yet it is the most real. And then there is the dream world, the least understood of the three. The dream world is the bridge between the other two. The secrets of the spirit world are brought to the waking world over the dream world's bridge. Though this is far from an easy task. The dream world's stories are told in a language that is hard to understand. And they are written in ink that is difficult to read in the waking world.

He heeds his master's words: *A dream is not to be taken lightly. A dream is a powerful ally, coming to your aid. A magic tale, written in invisible ink. A golden thread, tying together the worlds.*

PRAEDA

YOU ARE AT A YARD SALE. Tables are set up on a sprawling, lush green that covers an entire hillside. Not the typical fold-up, garage sale variety tables, but substantial pieces of furniture, antiques. Some more ornate than others, each covered with some type of cloth, from tattered linen to rich velvet. Candles, feathers and books are arranged on every surface. Along with all manner of stones and jewels. Each table is surrounded by buyers and sellers, bartering. Scattered among the tables are makeshift living rooms. Handwoven rugs from India and Afghanistan, rolled out on the grass, set the frame for each open room. Each space is anchored by colorful high-back chairs, couches, and settees arranged in clusters. People of all size and skin color sit together in these outdoor rooms, chatting enthusiastically, smoking from hookahs, drinking tea. You wander curiously through this mélange and then across the grass to the edge of the green where there is a steep cliff, overlooking a meandering river. The edge of the river is littered with broken bits of terra cotta, a living history of countless cups of chai.

You turn back to the gathering on the green and in a blink you are sitting in a dark purple chair, speaking to an old woman in pale blue robes, who hands you a cup of tea and asks you if you can see. *Of course I can see*, you think. But before you can answer out loud, she leans towards you and points her index finger to the middle of your forehead, then touches the spot lightly. The instant she does, a hole in your forehead opens up and the solid surface that was your skin ripples around her finger like water. At the same time, you see thousands of people in white robes standing about on an invisible plane, which stretches out beyond the horizon. One of them, a beautiful woman with sparkling green eyes and brilliant red hair, stands in front of you and bends down to speak. *Like what you see?* She says. And before you can answer, the old woman removes her finger and you are back in the outdoor living room.

Unceremoniously, the old woman asks what you have to trade. You look at your empty hands and think for a second. *This*, you say, as a deck of cards materializes in your right hand and you send an arc of cards through the air and into your open left hand, bridging the space between.

Card tricks, she huffs, and waves you off.

You shrug, finish your tea and excuse yourself. *She doesn't understand*, you say to yourself. *Sight is not the same thing as vision.*

Without bridges, there are no connections. Without bridges, there are only chasms. Without bridges, there are only longings. We cannot wait for the land to flatten and the stream to narrow before we seek to cross.

CHARYBDIS

LIFE MOVES BUT IT IS HARD TO SAY in which direction. Maybe it only crosses dimension. Maybe nothing is linear. Maybe all is perfectly still and there is only the traverse of the mind, in a spiral, through parallel worlds. Maybe what we see is only a trick of the brain. Maybe time only exists because of clocks, their hands moving around a fixed center to keep us focused, aging. Or maybe it's all a dream.

I wake up as the plane touches down in the dark at Indira Gandhi International Airport in New Delhi. There's nothing like air travel to scramble context. Climb inside a giant metal tube in one world and step out hours later into a completely different reality. It's a lot like dreaming, but in reverse.

In a dream, it's the dream world that is foreign (even if it makes some sense while you're there), but you wake up to a familiar world. When you travel to the other side of the planet, the world you wake up in is the one that doesn't make sense. Absolutely everything is different, the people, their clothes, their voices, and their skin. The streets are not recognizable, nor the vehicles and buildings that line them. The air you breathe smells and feels different. And there are even colors that never cross borders. I was told, by others who had been here, that nothing could prepare me for India. If air travel is crossing dimensions, going to India is traveling through time.

I walk off the plane tired, stiff, and probably still a little drunk. Though reality is so skewed I can't really tell. I wait on the concrete platform with the crowd of other passengers. After about half of them have claimed their bags, I start to get that feeling. That unmistakable mixture of hope and fear. Even if the airlines have never lost a single bag of yours, what if you're in India when it finally happens. After almost all the good people waiting have spotted and retrieved their luggage, my backpack finally shows up. I do my best to act like I was never worried, collect it and head towards a doorway where I see others exiting.

After a twelve-hour flight, in which the numbers of passengers alone means the restrooms are practically inaccessible, I need to make a brief stop before the next line. Since I don't read Hindi, I'm careful to watch which door the men are coming out. Inside the doorway there are tiny rooms with holes in the floor and buckets of water set beside the holes. This has been explained to me. Pour with the right, wipe with the left. I balance my backpack carefully in one corner while I attend to one part of being human which, even in the relaxed standards of the twenty-first century, isn't considered part of polite conversation. The simple act of defecation, its absolute ubiquity, its undeniable unpleasantness, along with its inescapable necessity, ought to keep us from thinking too highly of ourselves. It ought to lend towards humility and compassion for our fellow humankind. But somehow it doesn't. Especially in Western society, where we are numbed to these things through our surgical sterilization of almost everything. (I confess I did bring hand-sanitizer with me, so I'm not abandoning Western life entirely.)

Nevertheless, emerging from the doorway, I feel proudly initiated. An older Indian man spies me coming out of the stall and gives me a nod. I imagine it is a nod of approval. It doesn't occur to me that there might be Western toilets around the corner. And I'm not sure I would have sought them out in any case. In my mind, I went into the restroom a sheltered Westerner and I came out a traveler of the East.

I stand in the cattle call through customs and then find my way to the money exchange counter. The one other backpacker on the flight, an Aussie, walks past me while I'm collecting my rupees. For some reason he stops to wait on me. He gives the customary *g'day*, asks where I'm from and if I've ever been here before. Says this is his third trip here and that there are rooms at the airport we should use, because Delhi's not a place to try to negotiate at night. Better to stay here until dawn. (Which, as it turns out, isn't really that far away.)

We search for these guest rooms for some time, bouncing from this airport guard to that, being ushered in different directions until finally we get the same answer from more than one source: the rooms are under reconstruction and not available. We find a lone tea stall and, sitting on the concrete floor near the stand, drink what may be the worst cup of tea in all of India. While we sit there, sipping from paper cups and considering our temporary fate, we resign ourselves to looking for a place to just wait out the night, maybe even get a nap.

Turns out, the only place this is possible is the floor of a waiting area, where, unfortunately, a television hanging from the ceiling is playing what must be a Hindi soap opera. Actors and actresses are variously singing, screaming and crying in no certain order. The volume is set as if there were only two choices: mute and so loud someone on the other side of the airport could hear it over the din of a thousand voices.

We sit down on the bare floor, unzip our packs and rifle through our meager belongings. I roll up a jacket for a pillow and he covers himself with a long-sleeve shirt. I follow his lead and wrap my arms through the straps of my pack before I lay down.

* * * *

Sometimes I imagine the planet is a really big art gallery and my life is an impressionist painting. If I stand too close, it's all a blur, just smears and dots of color. To really see it, I need room enough to stand back and take it all in. I'm hoping India is far enough away to give me that perspective.

I understand that the world is messed up. Maybe it has always been messed up. If so, this time is no different. There are school shootings, corrupt politicians, environmental disasters, and prejudices that sometimes morph into genocide. The systems are rigged by the super rich, the food is poisoned, and God tells people to kill those who don't believe as they do. God sometimes tells their perceived enemies the same thing. Maybe God just likes to fuck with us. In any case, it does seem that lately things have sped up a bit. Maybe it's just to match the ever-increasing speed of our computers. But the disasters appear bigger, the hate stronger, and the squeeze on the everyday man and woman a little tighter.

I've asked a lot of people, read a lot of books, studied a few masters, sought the counsel of teachers, even been to a shrink, and I've yet to find anyone who can give me an acceptable answer to the question of why we're here. And while I'm pretty sure it is more than just to build a decent retirement plan or to collect a fleet of digital gadgets, most days I feel no closer to a cohesive answer than when I started with these questions. Every answer can be followed by another question. For example, if the answer is *we are here to evolve*, then what is the purpose of evolution?

It could be there is no universally ubiquitous right answer, of course, maybe not even any ultimate reality. It could be there is only what you believe. But how do you even know what that is? I think that's why I've come all the way here, to figure this out. In a way, I needed to take myself completely out of context, to meet myself somewhere out here on the other side of the globe. And then hopefully to come to terms with myself and my relationship to everyone else, everything else, in a way that helps me get out of bed, and then keep my footing once I'm on the floor.

I'd like to blame my sometimes dodgy footing on something concrete, like bad footwear. At least then I'd know that what I'm looking for is simply a place that sells better shoes. You don't need a degree in subatomic physics to figure that one out, and you don't need enough wealth to afford your own guru, either. I need something a simple guy like me can know is real, something to hold onto in the dark, a handrail for the psyche, if you will. A concrete image that won't slip from my fingers and float away as soon as I wake up. Something that won't dissolve in water or melt and dry up when the sun comes out.

Like most idealists I find temporary solace in feel-good theories of redemption. But nothing lasts. Usually sooner than later the Earth shifts again. And I end up lying in bed and wondering whether everything I've ever been told is a lie. *Lie* is perhaps not the right word. When people said *the world is flat*, that wasn't really a lie. Maybe people just don't know. I'm not sure whether it scares me more to think that people just don't know or to imagine that some of them know and are just complicit in some grand game of hide and seek. Of course, it's also possible they don't know and are just pretending they do. That would be lying, I suppose.

*   *   *   *

Speaking of scrambled context, I wonder what I'll think when I wake up here. That I'm dreaming? That's assuming I can actually go to sleep, on this cold concrete floor, with the nonstop Hindi scream-a-thon, nervous that as soon as I'm unconscious, someone will steal my backpack, effectively hijacking the plane headed to my original high-spirited destination of *Finding Myself* and forcing an emergency landing in the grass field of *Good Luck Finding My Way Home*. If I do sleep, the dreams should be interesting.

LE BATELEUR

THE FIRST NUMBERED CARD IN THE MAJOR arcana is called *Le Bateleur*, the Juggler. Also known as the Magician. He wears white robes accented by a red cloak. Before him is a table holding numerous items, including cups, coins and swords. His right hand is pointed up at the sky and his left down at the ground. In his right hand, he holds a wand. An uraeus floats like a halo over his head, a snake swallowing its tail wraps his waist, and he is surrounded by a garden of roses and lilies.

The Magician is a master of illusion. He is the bridge between spirit and flesh. And his tools are the same as the alchemist's: earth, wind, fire, water, and their corollaries: mind, heart, body, and soul. He teaches that what you believe is real is but a dream. Your life is a show, a juggling of elements, filled with traps for the unwary, and controlled by the wise. Only the Magician can lead the Fool out of the cave and along the first steps of his journey.

–THE BOOK OF MYSTERIES

SCYLLA

THE MONK WAKES FROM A DREAM into a world of mists and thunderclouds. The clouds play children's games with him. They show him dissolving images of yaks and sheep, serpents and hawks, angels and dragons. He closes his eyes and the clouds count to ten. He opens his eyes and they look for him. He breathes in the outside world. He breathes out the song of himself.

A fog envelops all that he cannot see. Above and below are confused into one. The clouds are made of roots and rocks. The land is air and water. The whole universe is a kind of living foliage. One that shapeshifts from deciduous compost to dragon lizards, from a muddy terrain to a marsh of leaches, from painted flowers to poisonous frogs, from sinewy roots to slippery eel. The rain is the master of all these illusions.

His physical body and all that it carries are rain-drenched and heavy. He has traveled for many days, protected from these elements only by the woolen clothes he wears. The long journey, filled with every hardship imaginable—swarms of insects, poisonous snakes, impossible terrain, hostile natives—has made his legs strong and his back sturdy, though it does not deter the pack he carries—an awkward appendage he has gradually grown used to—from its clumsy way of being.

The fog mandates that he see no further than the tree just before him. He moves in deliberate, steady paces. As if only his feet know the way, and they must direct his eyes, his mind. His master reminds him, *Life must be taken a step at a time. All else is madness.*

A crescendo of birds and beasts and wind and water fills every crevice of space around him. Still, his mind finds room to shelter a faint echo. A sound so slight it could be imaginary. A ghost who remains just out of sight, ready to disappear at the threat of being seen. The sound is the voice of a great waterfall. A bridge he must cross between worlds. He moves faithfully in the direction of its call.

The difficulty of his journey cannot be overstated. And he knows it is useless to dwell on such things. He knows that holding a focus on hardship only exaggerates its pain, gives it more attention than it deserves. *Always beauty must be held in the heart,* his master's memory reminds him. Filling the mind with trouble leaves no room for beauty there either. *We think our world into being.* Holding onto misery only brings more misery into focus. *All possibilities exist.* But the mind has only room for one thing at a time. He focuses on his gratitude for the shelter of the fog and the coolness of the rain.

Though this journey is the reason for his incarnation, he travels not simply for his own transformation. When he gets to where he is going, he will unlock a door for others. He will create a passage through which all generations may step into a new age.

*   *   *   *

He is interrupted gently by his master's voice. *What do you dream?* His master asks. *I dream the land and I are one,* he answers. He finds a crack in the fog and holds the light that slips through it. For the moment, this splinter of light is his stillpoint. It is his foothold on this murky passage.

PRAEDA

THE RED HAIRED WOMAN LEADS A YOUNG OX along the top of the high fortress wall in front of you. Like the other oxen on the wall, including the one you are leading, her ox is an illusion. The beast itself is real enough. As are the colors of paint on its sides, the rope she uses to lead it, and the wall itself. Still, these things are not what they seem.

Your prosperous village is under siege from an ambitious rival. It is a desirable conquest because of its rich soil, abundant water, and thriving trade. By painting the oxen and parading them atop the fortress walls like this, the villagers show defiance to their attackers. The painted oxen say without speaking, *You will not starve us out.*

As the battle wages on, though, the village's abundance has begun to wane. With rations becoming exhausted and the numbers of oxen dwindling, the woman with red hair appears at the base of the wall and gestures you down. With a pail of water and a cloth, and without explanation, she begins scrubbing the paint off the sides of your ox. Then she pats it dry and starts to paint a new design on it, using different pigments.

You continue to walk the remaining oxen along the high walls as before. But to hide their dwindling numbers, after each one is displayed, you and the other villagers quickly wash it, paint it with different colors, and parade it again. This has become a full time endeavor, as important as fighting the actual battle.

Eventually, the illusion works, and the attacking army retreats in defeat, suffering starvation and unsustainable losses of its own. Things are often not what they seem. And then, sometimes they are. The trick is to learn what is real.

CHARYBDIS

SOMETIMES I HAVE TROUBLE TELLING my dreams from reality. The farther I travel from some experience, the more unsure I am that it actually happened. Just like a dream, the closer I am to it, the more sure I am that it's real.

Where is the line? How can I trust that my image of the world is not a trick of the brain? That the external world is certain and the internal is imaginary? What if it's the other way around? What if the things I rely upon are actually made of air? Why is it that five people in a room witnessing the same event will have sometimes dramatically different accounts of what happened? Could there ever be such a thing as an objective truth?

I read a news story before I left the States about a man who regained his sight after having lived without it for decades. What he discovered was that his brain had forgotten how to see. He had perfect vision, but his eyes didn't work. Things he could do effortlessly when blind became frustrating and laborious. Familiar objects became foreign, as if he awoke one day with a profound form of amnesia. Simply picking up a cup of coffee from the table took an extraordinary effort.

In a blind world, things like shape and texture are everything. So visual images meant almost nothing to him when he regained sight. In short, he was forced to create a whole new relationship between himself and every other object in his world. Maybe the rest of us could use this kind of radical perspective shift. Maybe it would help us see ourselves and the world more clearly. More and more I get the feeling that I really don't know anything, that I've been sleep walking since I was a kid.

I had an experience when I was in Europe a while back, it's known as a kundalini awakening. I was in an ancient underground chapel, meditating, when these flashes of light shot up from the base of my spine towards my head. My whole body was filled with a surge of electricity. I know, it sounds crazy, but unlike some things, I'm pretty sure this happened. Anyway, around the same time, I started having these dreams.

In one series of dreams, I am a lion. And I'm going about doing lion things. And when I wake up, I'm sometimes shocked to find myself in human form. For an instant, I think I'm dreaming. I think I'm a lion dreaming that I'm a man. Eventually, I get up and make coffee and brush my teeth and somewhere along the way I settle on a reality where I'm not a lion.

I guess my point is, if I can have dreams that I believe are real, especially while I'm in them, how's that any different than what is happening right now? How's it any different from what I believe is reality?

When I was a child, I secretly believed that the world I knew while I was asleep was the real world and that my waking life was really just a dream. I've set down that idea for long spaces at a time, but it always has a way of catching my attention again, of reminding me it's still on the shelf, with the other forgotten distractions. I think it hangs around because I know there's something to it. We dismiss and forget many of our childhood notions at our peril. The world is as big as our ideas of it.

Despite the vividness of some of my dreams, it's usually hard for me to remember them with any consistency. Even the ones I remember have gaps in them. Sometimes large ones. Sometimes they are mostly gaps. Given what little information I am able to collect about the dream world, how can I really know anything about it?

Whatever some people might say, it seems to me that a world in which I can fly, bend space and time, and meet with people who have been dead for years, deserves more consideration than it gets. If I weigh the waking world on one side of the scale and the dream world on the other, which one is more substantial? Doesn't a world of endless possibilities seem more likely to contain the whole of our lives than the fraction of the world that we call real?

*　　*　　*　　*

I wake up on the floor. So I must have slept. And I probably incorporated the screaming Hindi television shows into my dreams. But I don't remember them.

My friend from Down Under pulls himself upright and rests against his backpack. It is surprisingly peaceful in here. No television opera, no bustling crowds. Just the sleepy morning stretch of the slender light of dawn. Through the glass walls we see the city start to wake up. Hungry taxi wallahs are already lining up outside. Their scurrying about reminds me of watching an ant colony under glass. I watch our packs while the Aussie goes outside to find us a ride.

I'm a pretty confident traveler, but he insists that I beware of thieves. Not the type you'd imagine, thugs lurking in alleyways or pickpockets. Apparently, there's a whole sub-economy here based on scamming tourists. For instance, there are more than a few taxi drivers who are paid to take you only to certain hotels, no matter where you tell them you want to go. So make sure you know where you're going, set the price for the ride before you get in, and don't pay a rupee more than agreed when you get out. It helps to know that there are generally three prices for everything: the Indian price, the Westerner price, and the naive tourist price.

The Aussie comes back in and says he found a ride for 150 rupees. *That's about three dollars and fifty cents U.S.*, he says, *we can split it.* So we grab our bags and he leads us through the tangle of cars and rickshaws crowding the pavement outside the airport doors. He scans the faces of the drivers until he finds the right one. We put our backpacks in the trunk and jump into the backseat. Next to the driver sits another man, whose purpose is unclear.

Even though the Aussie was specific about where we need to go, a short distance into the drive he realizes we're going in a different direction. He sits up and says no, this doesn't look right. He explains that we're not going to a hotel, we need to go to the train station. (We're not actually going to the train station of course. This is the trick the Aussie devised in self-preservation, because the place we want to go is near the train station. But if the driver and his friend in the front seat know we need a room, we won't get to where we're going.) The conversation escalates and the Aussie yells at them to stop the car and let us out. We get out, open the trunk and take out our backpacks. He throws 100 rupees on the ground in front of the driver. The driver is indignant and says he'll call the police. The Aussie tells him to go ahead, he'll be happy to report him. The driver calms down noticeably and says the police won't be necessary, that this is an acceptable fee for the distance they drove us.

We walk a couple of kilometers, ask a few people for directions to the Paharganj, and make sure we get the same story from more than one person. The Aussie says that rather than look ignorant, most locals will just point in a direction, even if they don't really know how to get to where you want to go. I'm starting to wonder what kind of shape I'd be in if I hadn't met him.

There really are cows wandering the streets in India. Lying down in the middle of traffic. And pigs eating all manner of trash, including what the cows leave behind. Because nothing goes to waste here, locals also take advantage of the cow patties, scooping them up and forming them into flat, round disks which they then stick to the outside walls of their houses. When the patties dry, they are peeled from the walls and burned as cooking fuel in the open fire pits inside their huts. This is India's recycling program.

Eventually we find the Paharganj, and along with it, a string of guest houses for backpackers. Crowded with cafés, chai stalls and spice wallas, the Paharganj is also the area's main bazaar—where the locals sell all types of handmade goods, saris, and shawls, as well as a trove of souvenir items. Bridging the past with present, it sits right between Old Delhi and New Delhi. If you're a Buddhist, you might think of it as the middle road, to a Catholic, maybe it's purgatory. For me, it's the perfect place to explore the in-between world of the land of dreams.

We're here before anything is open and roll-down steel doors line the whole street. It looks like a long strip of storage units. Adding to the scenery, there are crumbling brick facades and outdoor urinals. An old man sleeps on a rope bed in an abandoned structure without a roof. And in the middle of the street a large pile of garbage has collected for so long it has become a traffic median. Several pigs feast on the spoils. And there is no way to describe the smells. The Aussie is walking a couple of paces in front of me, but he turns and grins as he looks at me. *A little culture shock?* He asks. I nod reluctantly.

After walking around to a half dozen guest houses and asking questions at each, the Aussie is satisfied with one. For what the taxi ride should've cost, we get rooms for the night. After we check in and clean up a bit, we meet in the café on the ground floor and order up some omelets and chai. I can't believe there's actually a café in this place. The Aussie complains about the prices a little, 60 rupees for an omelet, but the food is way better than the walk in would indicate. And I begin to learn that cost is relative to place. He says I have to forget what things cost in the States and learn what they are worth here, so I don't get ripped off. It becomes an art for backpackers. Some even take it to extremes, like opting to sleep on the open roofs of guest houses, rather than pay for a room. These frugal purists will haggle over the price of almost everything, not satisfied until they know they've chiseled the profit margin down until it's see-through.

There's another conversation that often gets layered over the one about what things are worth in India. It's the one about what things *should* be worth. Should the world be flat? Should money be the same everywhere? And what does that do to culture? Some would say America has homogenized too much already. Leave things as they are. Others would say that's just veiled xenophobia, that these people deserve a higher standard of living. I'm on the fence. But I don't have a lot of money, either. And this is one of the few places left in the world where a guy like me can still do this kind of traveling.

None of this money-talk matters to me right now though. All the excited anxiety of travel, all the wondering if the planes will be on time, if me and my luggage will both get to where we're heading, if I'll be able to figure out how to get around once I get there, all that's gone. I'm there. Or rather, here. Unless of course, this is a dream.

LA LUNE

Number eighteen in the major arcana is called *La Lune*, the Moon. The moon rises between two towers, one light and one dark. In the foreground, the moon is reflected in a pool of water. A path leads from the water, winding between the towers and into the mountains in the background. Near the water, on either side of the path, a dog and a wolf bay at the moon.

The subconscious holds many valuable secrets. The reflection on the surface of the water is often mistaken for the mysteries that lie beneath. Likewise, the reflection of the moon is mistaken for its own light. In the quest for wisdom, each person must emerge from the illusions of the world and begin the journey towards the sacred mountain.

–THE BOOK OF MYSTERIES

SCYLLA

FROM TIME TO TIME, the world finds itself broken. At these times, all the magic that came before gets packed away. And those who carry it from place to place batten things down. What is left explodes. Into a billion tiny stars. And the light and the dark lose their separateness once more.

A space opens up during this time. A space held by the arms of eternity. In this time and space, in this corridor of eternity, the ants move. The monk knows something of their task.

Sometimes a journey is not about the traveler. It is not about a destination. It is about the bringing together of worlds. It is about lighting a path.

The ants journey not because of hunger, not to escape the rains, not driven by instinct or survival. They travel because they know the underworld. They know how to cross dimensions. They live between the worlds. Darkness becomes them and they are not frightened by the light. They are the carriers of the thread. When the world is broken above and below, inside and out, they are charged with mending the wounds in the dark, those left raw by the light. They are charged with building the new world. So we can start again.

He follows a thread that looks like theirs. Though he is above ground. Though his mission is not to wait until the world ends, but to find a way to the other side before it does. To prop open the door before it can be locked. To tie a suture before the fatal wound is made. To let in the moonlight before the sun is allowed to rise.

PRAEDA

THE NORTH AXIS OF THE EARTH is shifting away from the great fish of Pisces and towards the constellation Aquarius, the water-bearer, while the South Axis is pointing towards Leo, the great lion. This new configuration signals the return of an ancient messenger. Born of an order of lions known as the Kali Dasa Felidae, these messengers have an ancient pact with humans. When the old world is crumbling away, the lions will come to lead humankind across a new bridge.

The Kali have roamed the world for as long as memory reaches backwards. In India, the stone images at Mahabalipuram record their legacy as keepers of the secrets of Atlantis. And in Africa, from time to time, these lions appear in their purest white form, in a land called Timbavati, on the Nile Meridian, the meridian of First Time. This is one of those times.

*   *   *   *

There was once a Moon Goddess who marked the seasons and had the power to speed up, slow down, and suspend the movement of time. She seduced the seas to rise, the rivers to swell, and the wolves to sing her anthems at night. Because the powerful sun god coveted her seductive light, she devised a way to diffuse parts of her essence throughout the world. She found hiding places at the tops of mountains, the sources of rivers, and caves beneath the sea. And she chose a lion and a lioness, *Circa* and *Siri* to carry pieces with them. These were the ancestors of the Kali tribe.

Though it is said that the moon gift exists in the bloodline of every descendant of the tribe, every so often a new lion is born who carries the moonlight in its eyes and whose task it is to lead the Kali into a new age. It is not known how this gift transcends continents and shows up in the white lions of Timbavati when it is their time. The Great Mystery prefers to leave some stories untold.

* * *

In the light of the full moon, Mahatru, the ancient lion, watches you from his rocky perch as you skulk across the desert landscape.

The sand floats over the dunes like giant silk scarves, whispering just above the surface of the horizon. You travel at night, to avoid the heat of the sun, but also because lions are nocturnal by nature. Still, each new breath of wind washes over you like a wave of dry water.

Driven by some invisible force, you move without any true aim or direction. Simply placing one foot in front of the other in front of the others. Making a single line of prints in the sand. Pacing in one direction. Shedding what is already irretrievably behind you.

At the base of the rocks, you drink from a small stream and then begin to climb. When you reach a crest where you can survey the valley, you stop and lie down beneath a small tree. Exhausted, you quickly fall asleep. When you awake, you hear a voice:

Welcome.

You rise, standing curious and alert.

I am pleased to see you have begun your journey, young Aragon. What journey? You ask.

There are paths that some of us must travel. The older lion continues, without ceremony. *Not of the design of ancient societies or traditions. Not because they are well worn or provide a guaranteed passage. But because they belong to us.*

How do you know my name? What path are you talking about?

I cannot describe your path to you. Or tell you where it will lead you. I can only tell you stories of my own journey. I can share stories of others I have known and the legends that have been handed down.

You stand speechless.

This is your time, Aragon. You left your pride because somewhere inside your lion's heart you have an idea that something greater is waiting for you. You don't know what that something is, yet. But you have the sense of it. And it is strong enough to make you cast aside the security of your pride to go in search of it.

The elder lion then walked out of the shadows, as if materializing. *Let me explain, my name is Mahatru. I am your guide. Please, come with me, there is much to tell.*

CHARYBDIS

LATELY, I'VE BEEN HAVING THESE DREAMS where I'm in the middle of a jungle and I'm looking for something, some place, some time. Though I'm not sure what—or where—or when—it is. I am older, wiser, more surefooted. It seems that my quest is not just a personal one. At the risk of sounding dramatic, I have a sense that the world is at stake.

I had this thought this morning as I was waking up. How is it we get to and from the dream world? If all things are connected, then the dream world must be connected to the waking world somehow. What is it, then, that binds the two? What is the bridge, the connective tissue, the path from sense to chaos and back?

I don't know the answer to that, but I have this theory of dreams I've been working on. Monsters, of one kind or another, are common in dreams. And there's all this stuff in history, mythology, and psychology about monsters and demons and the courageous heroes who fight them. But I don't think fighting monsters is all that courageous. I think the ultimate act of courage is standing still in the face of a monster. Courage is looking closely enough into its jaws to see it for what it is: an illusion. The monster isn't real. It's your fear of the monster that is real. And just about anything in life can look like a monster if the light is just right.

Trying to figure out what is real is full-time work. Even more so, figuring out what matters, what is essential. I've been told I shouldn't think about these kinds of things so much. That I shouldn't constantly be searching for these kinds of answers. That I shouldn't be such a malcontent, because I have a really good life with nothing to complain about. No school shootings in my history, no suicide bombings, no waterboarding. It's true, there are people who are starving all over the world, people living in war zones, people being made to cover themselves from head to toe and obey misinterpreted scriptures. People who never know love. It is also true that I'm a bit of a malcontent. But that doesn't mean I should stop questioning. And it doesn't mean I'm not right about my belief that desire matters. That it is essential even.

Some Buddhists say we should liberate ourselves from desire. But I believe that's got to be a problem of translation. Not all desire is bad, is it? Shouldn't desire be qualified? Shouldn't there be a distinction between pure greed or obsession and healthy wants or even passion? I mean, isn't the Buddhists' quest to liberate themselves and others from sorrow another form of desire? Of passion?

I believe we should demand the things our souls need. And not compromise. Not push these desires to the slagheap because we've been told they serve no useful purpose in our adult lives. Not tell our souls to go to their rooms because we are having this party for adults called life, and they will just be in the way because we'll be talking about things the soul wouldn't understand anyway. Not say it's okay if we aren't granted these things we need, because other people's lives suck too.

All of life is constantly in motion. Desire keeps us moving. Desire inspires us to be brave, to dream, to create. Desire is our divine connection with the creative force of the universe. Desire also drives me to get outside right now, to connect, to start the next chapter, to let my curiosity roam free through this place and its people.

*   *   *   *

The Aussie dons his flip-flops for the walkabout, but I remember the state of the road walking in here and opt to keep my close-toed shoes on. Just an hour later and the Paharganj is completely transformed. The stalls are elbow to elbow with throngs of people, mostly locals, but also backpackers. I should probably tell you that many backpackers prefer to be called *travelers*. They believe this title sufficiently distances them from *tourists*, and somehow, I suppose, makes their experience more authentic. There is a legitimate point in there somewhere, but it also seems a little pretentious and delusional. I think *backpackers* is accurate enough, without having to pick a side.

I wander through the bazaar's maze of shawl wallahs, chai stalls, street food vendors, and all manner of other shops selling anything from shoes to incense to jewelry. The streets are so narrow there's barely room for a car to fit through. And yet there are all manner of vehicles here, including bicycles, rickshaws, and even a pair of camels weaving through the crowd. Along with so many turbans, saris, and children rushing past me, the visual onslaught of color and motion is almost paralyzing. Many of the children want to hold my hand or sell me something, or hold my hand so they can relieve me of something. But I am prepared for that much, with anything of value safely tucked away.

I want to capture this moment, to be able later to recall in detail the colors and the faces and the goods for sale, to describe these things to others. But my senses are overwhelmed, and I just can't hold all the fiercely raw beauty. At the same time, I'm struck by another sensation. One that whirls through my hair, fills my nostrils, and runs like a herd of gazelle through my veins. My recognition of it is so faint that it must whisper its name in my ear: *I am freedom*. Not the freedom we sell in America, not the creative freedom people like me crave, not even the free-love freedom of the Sixties. This is let go, cut-rope, free-fall freedom.

Upstairs in a café about twelve feet square and three stories high, on a corner where two channels of market-dwellers meet, the Aussie and I have a seat, order Limcas, and look down on the theatre below us. Down on the tangle of electrical wires which create a knotted trellis precariously tying together the buildings lining the streets. Down on a pulsing artery of Indian life. I am more of an observer than a participant here. An angel looking down on a fragile but beautiful creation I am not allowed to touch.

As I watch Indian street life unfold below, I am distracted by something out of place. It looks like a large reptile, some unknown creature slithering across the ground through the rickshaws and bicycles and loaded carts. In, out and around the hundreds of feet moving this way and that. The Aussie turns to see where my attention has been cast and we both stare until we decipher the shape of a mangled boy. His legs are twisted into question marks and he is dragging himself through the streets on his belly.

Without exception, the locals ignore him except to step around him or to move out of his path. Westerners move to the other side of the street when they notice him. Except for a young woman with dirty blonde dreads, who gets up from her seat at a chai stall to press some bills into his hand and then quickly returns to her companions. The Aussie tells me the boy is an untouchable, the lowest caste in India. Some believe if they touch him, or even pass through his shadow, they will become unclean. They also believe there is a natural order to this hierarchy which should not be disturbed. More shocking, the Aussie tells me that poor families will sometimes cripple their own children, in order to ensure they'll be able to make a living as a beggar.

I complain out loud about the cruelty of a system that locks a person into one category for life, with no hope for a better future, with no chance for social mobility, education, or prosperity. *Come on*, the Aussie says, *you think America is that different?* I start to argue, but after only a moment's reflection, realize it may not be. *America has its caste system*, the Aussie proclaims, *it just doesn't admit it. Think about it, celebrities, star athletes, and billionaires are America's Brahmin, the highest caste. Your politicians are your Kshatriya, the rulers. Your successful business owners are the Vaishya, or merchants. Almost everyone else, in other words most of you, are Shudras, or laborers. And then the welfare class and those in your overcrowded prisons are your Dalits, or untouchables.*

While I'm digesting this idea, the power goes out. But no one really seems to notice. I turn to the Aussie who says this happens all the time, sometimes several times a day, sometimes for hours at a time. Looking down at the confusion of black wires, tied together with tape and scrap wire, it's a wonder the grid is functional at all.

We finish our drinks and leave some change on the table. The power is still off, so we wander the streets, buy some veggie pakoras served in a newspaper cone, and check out more of the market's mélange. Though it is barely mid-day when we've made a complete pass around the bazaar, we surrender to the nagging tug of sleep and head back to the guesthouse for a nap.

As we're about to duck inside, I turn to see the faint shadow of the moon hanging low over the crumbling buildings. I am caught for a moment. As if I'm under her spell. And then it sinks in. Where I am, how far I've come, and that the journey has officially begun. I'm filled with nervous excitement, trepidation even. There is no knowing what's to come. Maybe I'll find a guru, shave my head, and never return to the States. Maybe I'll be killed in the crossfire of a religious war. Or maybe I'll lose my bag, my passport, and have to beg for food. Whatever my path, I must find the stillness and the courage to look it in the eyes and somehow not flinch, so I can see if it's real.

LES ETOILES

NUMBER SEVENTEEN IN THE MAJOR ARCANA is called *Les Etoiles*, the Stars. A naked young woman kneels with one foot in water and the other on land. She holds an urn full of water in each hand. She pours water from the urn in her right hand into the sea, creating ripples upon the water. The water from the urn in her left hand she pours onto the land, which flows into five tributaries. In the sky above the young maiden is a large yellow star, which is surrounded by seven smaller white stars. There is an ibis sitting in a tree behind her.

The universe is abundant and supports each of us. In order to see this, though, we must open all of our senses. We must be open to life's mysteries and its treasures. Only then will our spiritual life begin to flourish. We must take time for renewal, and have faith in our path.

–THE BOOK OF MYSTERIES

SCYLLA

THE MONK WAS CHOSEN FOR THIS PATH. Not because he is a great adventurer or a storied discoverer of mystical lands. Not because he is a master tracker, nor a student of plants and forests. He was chosen because of his ignorance of these things, an ignorance that forces him into a closer relationship with the land, the water, and the sleeping goddess who inhabits them.

His master taught him that knowledge is not the same thing as wisdom. Ignorance is different from unawareness. And awareness is more essential than a hundred skills. To be aware is to be open. And to be open is to know the path of every master who has roamed the earth. A master sees the illusion. A master understands the illusion. A master shapes and molds it, adds and subtracts from it, crafts its layers, and provides tools for its unveiling.

Though he has studied the teachings of the masters until they have become second nature, he is not a teacher. He is a tertön. It is his dharma to discover the teachings that remain hidden and to give them life. These teachings, known as *terma*, can take many forms. They may be writings. They may be ideas, insights, or even dreams. Or they may also take the form of a physical place or object that triggers a teaching in the mind or heart of a tertön.

So evolved was the relationship of his master Rinpoche to the elements, the Dorje, universal oneness, that he veiled 108 sacred

valleys from humankind. These valleys are a part of the terma
hidden by the Rinpoche, along with the cryptic maps for the
valleys, each written in ancient symbols and codes. The Rinpoche
timed the revelation of each, even naming the tertöns who would
one day reveal these treasures.

Each of the hidden valleys is a paradise unto itself, a cathedral
of nature. Each one waiting patiently for its time. Of all these
mystic places, there is one considered most sacred. This is the land
he seeks.

The Dorje is a sleeping goddess who inhabits this land. She is
one with it. She is a master dakini, a sacred muse, a shape-shifter,
a guardian of the mysteries of the self. With grace she walks in
all worlds, assumes all characteristics, is female and male, visible
and invisible, fierce and protective, omnipresent and nonexistent.
She is the guru and the consort, the Enlightened Buddha and the
Void.

The river is the blood of her veins, flowing through her chakra
centers. It begins in the exalted purple mountain of her crown,
descending over giant boulders into her throat, where it sings
the most beautiful song known on earth. From here it enters her
heart and encircles the peaks of her breasts, which are covered
in flowers known for their honey-sweet nectar. Then it continues
down through her navel in the valley of sweetgrasses and into
her secret place, the mountain of crystal lotuses. It is written that
upon entering the threshold of her secret place, all human veils
will be lifted and the karmic entanglements of thousands of years
will be erased.

Each of these centers is a lotus, unfolding with four layers of
petals. To enter fully into any one center, the tertön must move
through the four layers: the outer, the inner, the secret, and the
hidden layers. And to find the Dorje's secret heart, he must enter

through the crystal lotus mountain and into the heart of hearts of the land.

The Dorje's resting body bridges two lands. Her lower half, from her feet to her navel, is in one land. Her upper half, from her navel to her crown, lies in another.

He, too, must bridge these worlds, in order to find her. In order to unlock the door to her heart. In order to bring her sacred fire to the rest of humanity. And to use that fire to light up the starlight locked in everyone.

*   *   *   *

There is a sacred marriage between water and earth, Rinpoche taught. *Their relationship binds everything we know and trust. Earth holds space for water. Water nurtures earth's dreams. Their collective desires make life possible. Without their marriage, this world could not be. And we could not be of this world.*

Their story is our story, as well. We are the begotten ones. Our flesh is made of clay. Rivers run through our veins. Our lineage stretches from the ocean floor to the mountain crest. This is the beginning of knowledge.

The story of the union of earth and water is coded and kept hidden. Unless you know how to listen. Unless you know where to look. Then, each page of the story is revealed. Through the layers of earth and rock and fossil, on the leaves that fall from the trees, in the crystals that form in winter. Their messages are the maps that guide his journey.

PRAEDA

You LIE FAST ASLEEP FOR ONE OF MANY ETERNITIES. Floating in the nothingness. Drifting on an empty, endless ocean, resting on the countless coils of a giant snake whose name you have forgotten. While you rest, floating, drifting, at peace, eventually you begin to dream.

You dream of a new world to come, a new world to be birthed, a new dream to be dreamt. In the dream, a flower grows, a lotus from which the creator and the creation will unfold. From which light will begin to shine upon this vast dark sea, unveiling all the magic sleeping within. From this flower, infinite worlds and universes will be born. Each will contain a seed of light. And these seeds will light the heavens for all to guide their journeys by.

You are the dreamer, the creator of the creator. You are the protector. You are the restorer of order. You are the message and the messenger. Your name is Vishnu. And the world is your avatar.

CHARYBDIS

WHEN I WAKE UP, I decide to wander over to the train station, careful to trace my steps so I don't get disoriented. I'm not very good at keeping my directional bearings. I usually have to rely on visual clues that I pick up while coming or going.

If I were someplace else, say Munich or Paris or San Francisco, I wouldn't worry as much because I could jump on the metro or ask a taxi to take me back to my room. But here it seems I might only get to where the driver was paid by someone else to take me. I realize I'm probably being overly vigilant. But while this place is still wild and unfamiliar, I must try not to get too lost.

I walk the few blocks to the train station, passing several centuries of history all at once. There is an Internet café next door to a crumbling, windowless façade where a woman tends to her chapati fire. As with yesterday, there are cows and pigs and garbage everywhere. And yet, the streets are buzzing with people and traffic and brightly colored saris and headscarves. I wander among them in awe. I wonder if they can see me, if I am really here. The scene seems more like a dream than reality.

At the train station, things are far from spelled out. Just making it to the right room and finding the right form to fill out is an adventure. But my journey is young and I am patient to learn. I am given a train schedule, which is printed on newsprint and staple-bound. Reminds me of the class schedules I pored over every semester in college. There wasn't a condom ad right in the centerfold of the class schedule, but there probably should have been.

The Aussie told me to book a second-class seat, but I am nervous and check first class instead. The difference is only about twenty dollars. I'm slow to take to the idea of living as ludicrously cheap as apparently I can here.

When I finish at the station and find my way the short distance back to the Paharganj, I go in search of beer. I'm on vacation, after all. *Holiday*, as the Aussie says. I find a bar on a far end of the bazaar. I open the door and immediately feel like I've crashed an invite-only party. There are no backpackers in here, only angry-looking Indian men. But so many faces are staring at me I can't just turn around and leave. Luckily, I am accustomed to being somewhat uncomfortable in my skin, so I find a seat, immediately pull a book from my bag and disappear as best I can.

When the bartender approaches and indifferently asks what I want, I hastily order a Flying Horse, not wanting anyone's attention to linger on me for too long. They only have Fosters and Kingfisher, he says, looking annoyed. I take the Kingfisher, the Indian beer, knowing he expected me to choose the Fosters. When he brings the beer, I immediately slide a large bill across the table, not having any idea of the price. This, too, annoys the barkeep it seems, as he is forced to give me a lot of change in return. Maybe the locals all pay with exact change. I have no idea, but resolve to make better decisions about where I spend my time. I read the book and drink the beer, but I'm not really having fun. I'm just trying to save face by not leaving here too quickly.

Back at the guesthouse, the Aussie's girlfriend has shown up to meet him. She wants to go see the Taj Mahal, which is just about 30 miles from Delhi, in a town called Agra. According to

PAINTED OXEN | 61

the guide book, there's not many places you'd want to stay in Agra and the majority of buses going there are group tours, most of which include at least a night's stay. I've never been a big fan of the cattle call. Added to this, the Aussie heard about a poisoning scam from some backpackers who just came back from Agra. Some of the restaurants where the guided tours go were intentionally giving tourists food poisoning and then getting a kickback from the hospitals where they were taken for treatment. Given these dodgy options, the three of us decide to book a private car leaving first thing in the morning. Turns out, split three ways, renting a car for the day is less than the tour bus price.

The next morning the driver is there waiting before we have time to eat. We sneak in a quick breakfast anyway and load up. The car is called an Ambassador. It looks like a smallish 1950's throwback, and with a max horsepower of 42, it tops out at about 35 miles an hour. So we're not exactly bending time getting to Agra, but there's really no hurry, either.

The highway drive is a living lesson in the history of transportation. It is filled with buses, cars, and trucks of all sizes and ages, along with camels, bikes, motorcycles, and dangerously overloaded hay carts pulled by water buffalo. All sharing the same river of pavement. Add to this the daredevil vehicles, who get around the bottlenecks caused by this weird traffic coterie by crossing at the median cuts and driving into the ongoing traffic lanes, then zipping back over at the last minute. Lying crumpled on the side of the road are pieces of evidence that some don't make it back in time.

We pass an old man wrapped in linen sitting on a slat of wood high atop a cart pulled by two enormous oxen. Black eyes stare into the sun. The weathered skin of his face and hands, seared and deeply creased, shows through gaps in the gauzy fabric covering the rest of his body. I listen to the long horns of the oxen knocking into each other as they walk side by side, and to the whip cracking over their heads, which is attached to the weathered hand of the man wrapped in linen. All of these things sharing the same road with us.

Once in Agra, we go to the Red Fort first. The Red Fort is where Shah Jahal, the Emperor who had the Taj Mahal built, was imprisoned by his own son, who knocked him off his throne, but at least put him in a cell where he had a view of the Taj. The Red Fort is supposed to be a great place to take a picture of the Taj Mahal, because up close, you just can't get the whole thing in the picture frame. We're not getting one of those shots today, though. We've climbed up to the lookout, but the pollution is so thick you can taste it, and we can barely even make out the shape of the great structure. We walk around for a while checking out the Fort, a pretty amazing piece of architecture in itself, but the difference between the pictures of the Taj we've seen from here and the reality we find ourselves in leaves us a little disillusioned.

When we arrive at the Taj Mahal, the feeling I have is unfamiliar. This incredible structure took 22 years and 20,000 people to build. How do I react to touching something I've only seen in pictures and never imagined I'd stand beside. This is a problem with traveling for me. It's hard to take it all in, hard to be present enough to record the whole of it in my memory. Is it more than I imagined? Is it less? For those who live in Agra, the Taj is probably just another part of their lives. But for me, it is likely this is the only time I'll be here.

Again I arrive at the question of how to capture it. This is another popular debate with backpackers. The argument against taking photos is that you can either have an experience or you can record it, but you really can't do both. If you try to record an experience, you are not really capturing the moment; you are diminishing it. Or as someone put it, I can't see myself having a great conversation and stopping in the middle to take notes.

We have to take off our shoes before entering. This is the first I learn of this tradition. In all temples and most stores in India, this is expected. At a place like this, it's also a good idea to pay someone to watch your shoes. Or so the Aussie says. Looking around at most of the shoes next to ours, I see why.

It takes a minute to realize what this means: I get to walk barefoot through the Taj Mahal. Something I never expected. I've loved to go barefoot since I was a kid. I take off my shoes every chance I get. Even in college, I used to walk to class barefoot when it was warm, and happily endured the stares and comments from others. Suddenly, this small detail, being barefoot in the Taj Mahal, makes the trip here surpass all my expectations.

The Taj is actually a mausoleum, built by Emperor Jahal for his favorite of three wives. It sits on the banks of the Yamuna River, and legend has it that Jahal intended to build an identical Taj, in black marble, on the other side of the river, with a bridge between the two. Though we know that Jahal's son deposed and imprisoned him not long after the final construction, it is not known whether this interrupted his plans for a second Taj or if the whole idea of the black Taj is a romantic myth. Upon Jahal's death in 1666, perhaps as a way to make up for his Shakespearean deeds, his son had him buried next to his wife in the only Taj we know to be real.

It appears smaller than you'd think on the inside, but I linger for a long time anyway. I press my feet into the white marble and try to record the imprint of the smooth, white stone on my skin. There are no pictures allowed in here. So I get to test the no-picture-taking theory and make myself remember with photographic details this once in a lifetime view.

My companions leave the building before I do. But I linger, concentrating on the size, the feel, the calligraphy, even the spaces where the 28 types of precious stones were removed from the walls by the barbaric acts of occupying British forces. Eventually I take my leave of her and go outside to walk around the grounds and the spires. I take pictures now that I'm outside. I even sit down and pull out my notebook, but I can think of nothing to write. So I just sit. Still barefoot. Knowing this moment will pass too quickly. I repeat to myself a few times the guy's name who built this, Shah Jahan, it seems like an important thing to remember. So does the name of the queen for whom the Taj is named, Mumtaz Mahal, but her name is harder for me to remember. Before I am ready, the Aussie appears in the distance and waves me in.

Going back home, the traffic story is the same. Except that it's dark, and the dozens of roadside cafés, which I barely noticed on the way here, are now unmistakable. Florescent lights have been strapped to trees in front of each one, illuminating the whole make-shift world with their eerie alien glow.

We stop for a bite at one café. Being closer to the neon glare does not reduce its surreal factor. If anything, it accentuates it. I glance down the length of the highway, admiring the pattern created by the string of lights from all the other cafés. I wonder if people in outer space can see them. I wonder if they look like constellations to them. I wonder if they are creating myths around their shapes, to guide them on their paths.

If this is a dream, I hope I remember it.

LA PAPESSE

NUMBER TWO IN THE MAJOR ARCANA is called *La Papesse*, the Female Pope. Also known as the High Priestess. A woman draped in blue robes and wearing the crown of Isis is seated on a throne above a checkerboard floor. Under her foot is a crescent moon. In her lap is a book of sacred laws, and in her left hand are the keys to the secret doctrine, one gold and the other silver. Behind her is the Tree of Life, and on either side rise two pillars, one black and one white. A multicolored veil is stretched between the two pillars. Another veil partially covers the book in her lap.

Divine Wisdom acts as the gatekeeper to the Great Mystery. The whole truth is not revealed to the uninitiated. Without divine knowledge, only half of the mystery of being can be comprehended.

–THE BOOK OF MYSTERIES

SCYLLA

THE DORJE, the sleeping goddess who inhabits this land, has her own language. It is a language she has taught him over these long weeks they have spent together. It is not a human language, not text that can be written on a page. Her words sound more like fish who break her surface, rapids that run beside him with their rhythmic thunder, plants along her banks who sustain his being, and flowers that open him to the millions of hidden senses. She speaks a multitude of other words in this language only she and he know. Still many words remain that she has not uttered.

There are many other guides on his path. There are the leaves and the birds, the wind and the stones, the sun and the moon, the stars and the soil. Each of these has its own language to teach. And there are those, like the clouds and the rain, whose voices drown out all others.

A language is made up of words, whatever their shape. And a word is a living thing. It is an entity unto its own. Try to imagine a thought without words. Then try to imagine a word without thoughts. A word is a bridge. It is a wave of light and sound that spans the perceived distance between one thing and another. Words make access possible.

In the beginning was the word. And the word was split into infinity. All words, then, are part of the whole. Just as we are each part of the whole. There are individual words, as we are individual beings. *Each word carries with it the memory of the whole logos. Just as we each carry the memory of the whole universe.*

The moon speaks in slivers and halves. It has divided itself to stay in rhythm with the split-apart words. The moon is forever reincarnating itself, reinventing its language. The moon is the mirror of the sun. Though the sun has its own language, which the moon cannot speak.

It is important to remember that half the world is upside down. So it is with our thoughts. One's word for sun may be another's moon. Words grant freedoms beyond quantification. They bridge galaxies in a blink. And they bring back to us the stories of who and why we are. It is important to remember, though, that a word can never be more than half the moon.

His journey is often treacherous. Lined as it is with slippery surfaces and dangerous creatures. Each step must be taken mindfully. It is no different with each word spoken. Courage, humility, and trust in one's voice, these are the paths to understanding. Combined, they are the keys to unlock the oneness that words carry in their helix.

PRAEDA

You DREAM OF CAMELS. And also of wind and bells and dust and colorful headcloths. The young woman with brilliant red hair is here. She walks beside you, her white robe gliding along the dirt road, as if there were a pocket of air between her and the ground. Neither she nor the robe gathers any dirt as she moves along the dusty streets, in and among the camel drivers, speaking in tongues, exchanging coins, occasionally turning her face towards you.

She leads a single camel without a rope. Its reins rest loose on its shoulders. The camel's back is covered with a thick wool blanket, faded in color and frayed at the edges. And there are two leather saddlebags, filled with unknown provisions.

You follow her. She leads with grace. She appears neither coy nor aloof. Simply knowing, aware. A few strands of her hair are tied with leather strips on either side of her head. And in her left hand is a pouch made of bright blue fabric. She makes her way to a stall on the outskirts of the town. You join her at a small table where she is already pouring tea for you. She sets down the pot and then looks up at you. You don't know where you are, only that she is why you are here.

You want to know about the camel, she says. She speaks in a manner-of-fact way, but without a trace of arrogance. Somehow, she gives you the feeling of being understood without even having to speak. After she sips her tea, but before you can answer—or rather, because speaking seems unnecessary—she begins to explain.

The camel is the favorite of the High Priestess, who is the bridge between the darkness and the light. As the keeper of sacred wisdom, as the Goddess of the Moon, as the bearer of the crown of Isis, the High Priestess requires a vehicle to transport her gifts of abundance from the dream world. Camels are perfect companions for any pilgrimage. They are skilled guides and suited for long and difficult journeys. Also, something happens on the back of a camel. We begin to see things from a different perspective. And a new world opens up for us. One we didn't know existed.

She takes another sip of tea, then rises from her chair and gathers the camel's reins, slowly lifting them over the gentle beast's head. When finally you find the courage to speak, you ask, feebly, where she is headed with her camel. She turns back to you, a look of surprise on her face.

The camel is for you, she says, and hands you the reins.

CHARYBDIS

I WRITE WITH BLUE PENS NOW. Glass pens with little, painted, blown-glass animals at the top. I bought them from a little girl outside the walls of the Taj Mahal. I didn't realize how hard it would be to find pens here. I would have brought more with me. For years I used nothing but black ink. I don't know why, maybe it just seemed more substantial, made more of a statement. Maybe blue seemed too unsure of itself. Like I might as well have been writing with a pencil.

Walking away from the Taj, there's the usual throng of Indian children trying to sell us any manner of things. This one little girl catches my attention, though. And when I stop to talk to her, I find out she is selling pens. She hands one to me and asks if I want to buy it. I inspect it. It's quite an amazing thing, really, for a place where it's hard to find a pen at all. I joke with her for a minute and pretend to haggle over the price of one of them. Somewhere in the middle of this I remember that I actually need pens, so I buy the whole box. Twelve amazing little hand-painted, blown-glass pens, for 10 cents apiece or something ridiculous. So for the moment I write with blue pens. But they have a story behind them. Their story makes the ink more substantial I think.

*   *   *   *

I'm on the train to Jaipur. The one I booked in first class instead of second. Actually it isn't the exact same one, because technically I missed that one. This is one I booked after I arrived at the train station at the wrong time. I am sitting across from a well-dressed, middle-aged Indian couple. He is a dignitary of some type and she works for a bank. Unquestionably they are rich by Indian standards.

As a rule, Indians do not travel light it seems. The luggage at the Delhi airport was the largest I've seen anywhere. And my travel companions to Jaipur have no less than two large bags just for their tiffins (round metal food containers). I should clarify that I mean no disrespect. They are generous and kind to me. She feeds me several times during the train ride. And I am grateful for the food. Even so, when I'm so full I can no longer accept any more, even out of politeness, they continue to open more tiffins. I don't pretend to know with certainty the reason for this over-abundance, but it feels like a way to stave off the hunger that is all around them.

We engage in polite conversation for a while, and they are fascinating travel companions for their worldliness, their education, their perspective, and their abundance, but it is a long train ride, and I run out of things to say. Mostly I stare out the window, at a scene that would make Van Gogh blush. It's no wonder there's so much poverty in this country, all its wealth is invested in colors. The houses are painted in cheery shades of blue and peach and red and orange. And the countryside is painted in mustard blooms as far as I can see. There is a rapid rhythm of conversation throughout the train, but I understand almost none of it. Instead of being distracting, the rumble fills the space around me, holding a place for me to think.

We move on from village to village, fields of green and gold, foothills and scattered trees, bamboo and hay, brick and wall, thatch and canvas. And still more colors for which I have no name. Then another village and more unfamiliar colors I may never see again, along with silhouettes of camels and a red sunset that threatens to set fire to the horizon. There's a man riding a bike past a field of goats, two broken tractors, and a woman carrying a load of sticks on her head. These twilight scenes somehow remind me of Africa, though I've never been there, but as the sun tucks itself away for the night, I imagine I see the shadows of elephants.

*   *   *   *

We arrive in Jaipur after dark. In another surprise move of kindness and generosity, the dignitary from the train gets off with me, finds a rickshaw driver and pays him out of his own pocket. He gives the driver strict instructions where to take me, and gives me his personal number to tell him if the driver does not do exactly as instructed.

The hotel is wonderful. Though the floors are concrete and the bed not especially comfortable, compared to most backpacker rooms, it's the picture of luxury. And, for about seven dollars a night, I not only have my own bathroom, but a balcony with a view, as well as a restaurant on the roof, overlooking the city lights.

In the morning, I go for a walk through the Pink City. I wander the narrow, winding back roads, where the locals are. I stop and talk to strangers in their shops. I am desperate to experience the real India. If I could change the color of my skin and my eyes, I would. I stop for chai in a tiny stall, roughly the size of a walk-in closet, where I hand an old man wearing a dirty undershirt two rupees for a glass of tea as small as its price. The only place to sit is an unpainted board, twelve inches wide, six feet long and six inches off the ground. We smile and nod to each other, but neither of us speaks. I watch him stir his chai in a large steel wok, over a little fire. His pale red lungi, frayed at the edges, is also in need of a wash. I guess that he has no wife at home to take care of these details. It also occurs to me that this chai stall could be his home.

From my low perch, I watch the world as it passes by on these dirty side streets. There are no westerners in this corner of the city. Just locals going about their business. Weighing out brightly colored spices, walking back from the fish market, stopping at the paan shop, socializing over tea. Old men in lungis and flip-flops walking hand in hand and dirty-faced children who are all bright smiles and wild eyes. I am comfortable here. Sitting on this board, in this tiny chai stall, hidden away from the recognizable world. For the moment, I have disappeared.

*　　*　　*　　*

I meet a Brit back at the guest house. He's on his way home, after a six-month stint in Kerala working for an NGO. Like the Aussie in Delhi, the Brit proves invaluable in teaching me what I need to know to get by here. We go shopping for all kinds of things I don't really need, like silk shirts, saris, and jade statuettes, and others that I do, like sheets and lungis (which really aren't that different), shawls and soap. We spend hours upstairs in one shop owner's attic, drinking chai, smoking a hookah, and trying on racks of clothes, as the owner rolls out fabric upon fabric, and rug upon rug, for our perusal.

At night, we crash an Indian wedding. The Brit tells me the locals love it when westerners attend. It's supposed to be good luck or something. I'm skeptical, but it turns out it's true. In fact, they dote on us. From the moment we walk in, hosts in ceremonial dress bring us plate after plate of exotic food and pay us almost too much attention. You'd think one of us was the groom.

Weddings are a big deal in India. The father's ability to put on as big a party as possible for his daughter reflects his prominence in the community. Many of the men, both older and younger, engage us in conversation. Many of the questions are designed as bait for answers that will flatter the host. They also seem eager to preemptively defend the system of arranged marriages. A topic, of course, neither the Brit nor I would bring up on our own. Out of politeness, if not an innate sense of self-preservation, we manage to skirt the issue.

Two young girls bring us each a long-stemmed flower. But before we can thank them, they retreat to the sides of older, seated women. There are also several beautiful young women in attendance, but despite repeated attempts, I cannot catch the eye of even one of them. The Brit must have noticed my feeble efforts, because he whispers to me that the unmarried women here are forbidden from talking to us without an adult present. Also, he explains, the only reason for an introduction would be if the elders saw us as candidates for a similar ceremony of our own.

*   *   *   *

The air in Jaipur is even worse than Agra. Turns out my immune system is not up for the challenge, and by day three I catch a nasty cold. But I am determined not to let it intrude too much on my adventures. I take whatever cold remedies I can scrounge up, drink some chai, and pull on my day pack.

Other than the cold, the day starts out fine. I head out to get some pictures of a few touristy sights, places I haven't seen yet due to my general preference for the obscure. While sitting in a local food stall, a young Indian boy approaches me and asks if he can sit at my table. *Of course*, I say. I offer him tea and he accepts. He says some Westerners don't like to talk to Indians, and asks if I'm okay with him asking me questions. *This is a funny place to be for people who don't like talking to Indians*, I tell him. We talk while I finish my snack and then he invites me to meet some of his friends. I decide, it isn't as if I have any other place to be, exactly. And I am here to follow the thread of adventure where it leads me.

I go back to a flat, where three or four other teenage boys are hanging out. They order a round of chai for the room and quiz me about life in America. I play along for a while, but soon the talk turns to sex. Knowing the strict customs of much of India, I am uncomfortable having this conversation. I have no idea what kind of trouble I could stir up if I entertain their questions. As I attempt to steer the conversation in other directions, it turns out they have an agenda of their own. It soon becomes apparent that they are pawns in a game to get me to import (read: smuggle) jewels for them into America. I am promised a handsome cut.

And I thought the sex talk was uncomfortable. I haven't heard of this scam yet, but something doesn't feel right. Also, the cold is starting to take its toll on me and I am feeling worse and worse, so I try to excuse myself to go back to my room and take a nap. But instead of backing off, their pressure escalates. I am increasingly aware of the need to remove myself as delicately and as immediately as possible. While they are teenagers, they are not children, there are four of them, and I don't really know where I am or how easy it would be for me to leave, should I flatly refuse their offer. As a diversion, I decide to tell them a story about a dream I had:

I am on a bridge, an old stone bridge. A lush riverbank awaits on the other side. I'm not quite halfway across, but I notice as I walk that the bridge is not all there. It is not a new bridge, so it doesn't seem likely that it is simply unfinished. Despite the inevitable peril, I don't appear concerned about falling into the water. Just as I am approaching the edge of the bridge, a white beam of light appears over my head. More accurately, the beam is going straight into my head. The light fills my whole body and turns into a sparkling white mist. The mist then expands beyond my physical form, spilling out over the bridge and into the firmament, illuminating a thousand pathways on all sides of me.

When I am done, I stand up and say, *So what is the lesson here, boys?* Faced with blank looks all around, I answer for them, *Is it that there are always more paths for you to take than you imagine? Or is it simply that it is a bad idea to do mushrooms before going to bed? I'll let you decide.* And then I bow and say, *Until we meet again.* Never planning to see them again, of course. But this is not the end of it. They insist to know where I am staying so we can continue this conversation. And just as I am pondering the odds of my escape if I simply bolt for the door, a woman in a royal blue sari appears at the doorway. She gestures for the teacups and the tray, which the boys immediately fetch for her. Then she turns to me and says, *Jaipur is a wonderfully big city, I'm sure you'd love to see more of it than this room. Come with me and I'll tell you some things that aren't written in your guidebooks.*

L'EMPEREUR

NUMBER FOUR IN THE MAJOR ARCANA IS L'EMPEREUR, the Emperor. An older man with a long white beard sits upon a throne adorned with ram heads. A phoenix sits by his side. His legs are crossed in the shape of the number four. In his left hand is an orb depicting his influence over earthy matters, and in his right, an ankh, celebrating Life. He sits before a range of golden mountains.

The Pythagoreans believe the number four represents wholeness and completion. On this earthly plane, there are four seasons, four winds, and four primary elements. The figure on the throne has mastered the secret of creating order out of chaos, the trick to removing veils of mystery, and the art of manifesting ideas on the physical plane.

–THE BOOK OF MYSTERIES

SCYLLA

To STAY ON THE PATH, he must follow the echo. An echo is not the thing itself. An echo is something that is real, authentic, but not original. A reflection. A footprint. A trace of sound. A trail leading back to the source.

To hear the echo, he listens for his own footsteps. The echo is a gift, passed on to us by our ancestors many ages ago, to remind us of ourselves. To confirm our existence. To remedy our loneliness. Though we must be still in order to hear it. The echo is audible only if ego and soul are in balance. His master taught him to find his voice and to use it. The echo teaches us that we must also make space for listening.

The ears are the eyes of the dark, as the stars are the eyes of the night sky. With concentration, all things are possible. Through listening, he can know the seasons, the direction of the winds, and whether the eye of the moon is open and how much. We cannot see beyond the horizon, yet we know the world is there. Clarity comes through the mind's eye, not through the illusion of the looking glass, not through the flat reflection that gives no true depth or meaning to the life it pretends to reflect.

The echo is water's freedom song. As physical beings, we are confined by our illusions, our fears, our prejudices. Water knows no boundary. Though we may draw it on a map, say *this is where the water starts and where it ends*, it is not true. Water knows the way into the Great Mystery. It is not afraid of going underground. Water is not afraid of dams or dry creeks, bridges or brick walls. It is patient. Water understands time. It will find a way. Water is not afraid of bugs or snakes, worms or spiders, earwigs or scorpions. It coexists. He has learned of all of this by listening. To the words of his master. To the sounds of the world around him.

In this place he is seeking, water falls on rock. Sometimes in gushes or great floods. But also drop by drop. These drops have carved out a basin and in that basin these drops gather. Ages pass. While each new drop surrenders, the others celebrate by singing. The notes of their songs look to us like tiny, circular waves moving out in all directions. In one continuous motion.

This movement, this displacement of sand, this eternal patience, this is water's story. This is its dance. As these dillons silently sing their endless song, the reservoir swells. As he climbs up the steep path, as he stops to rest on a boulder, as he sleeps beneath the Aspen, the water is cresting. And letting go.

All the while, the echo of its surrender lingers just beyond the grasp of ordinary awareness. A secret whispered on the ocean. A vibration he has trained a lifetime to hear.

PRAEDA

In the beginning, it is always dark. And this darkness contains all potentialities, all possibilities of color, shape, form, texture, density, scale. To work in the dark, you must be able to hold your own light, and still be intimate with the darkness. Never approach it with trepidation or hesitancy. Never doubt your ability to find your way through the dark, for this is no way to begin. If the ground of your own heart is unprepared, no amount of skill will ever be sufficient to produce the results you seek.

Alchemy, the masters teach, is the process of linking the spiritual to the material. The alchemist is the bridge between the worlds. It is a process of working inside a mirror, knowing always that in the end, the part will reflect the whole. As inside, so outside.

You move into the darkness, wrapping it around you like a heavy cloak. You dive into it naked like a midnight swim, slip beneath its covers and invite it to envelope you, as a dream. You lose yourself in the richness of its mysteries. You start to become the darkness. It starts to become you.

Soon enough there will be heating and sublimating, distilling and watching. Soon enough there will be light and separation. But for now you allow yourself to be swallowed by the luxury of darkness. And to your great surprise, you find that you are surrounded not by blindness and ignorance, but by a vast knowing.

The darkness grounds you. And though you understand that eventually it will need to share its light, for now, you are comfortable wrapped in its blanket. You know the time will come when you must begin the process of turning over the darkness, of stirring and heating it. Of drawing out the light. And when that time comes, you must be patient, like a skilled lover. You must allow time for passion to build and then carefully control its release.

When you have applied just the right pressure, introduced the right heat at the right time, moved swiftly when called for, then slowed down as necessary. When you have coaxed the light from the center, up through the body, and offered a safe space for it to show itself. When the sun is resting beneath its horizon and the moon casts just a sliver to light the room, then the delicate white edges of your lover's curves will be revealed.

Just as the leafy stem grows up through the murky pond until it reaches the border of the worlds. Just as the broad leaves then stretch themselves out upon the surface. Just as, when the conditions are perfect, the graceful white lotus unfolds, showing itself. So when the alchemist has held steady and kept his faith, the white edges will appear, signaling the promise of change to come.

CHARYBDIS

Sometimes I wake up to find myself in what I call *the void.* Like the name implies, it is a feeling of great emptiness, but also of purposelessness, and its own brand of despair. It's kind of an existential free-fall. Maybe it has to do with something that happened in the dream world. But I can never recall what or even how. I can't use logic to escape the void. I can't rely upon hope. There is nothing that allows me to reason or think my way out. The only trick I have when this happens is to tell myself—against all logic, reason, and emotion—I won't feel this way forever.

I can't explain why I won't or how. But stored somewhere is the memory that I have been here before. The void is familiar in an odd, dark sort of way. Like a friend who supports your wallowing. I remind myself that I haven't always been here, and so somehow it will get better again. Something in me knows I will eventually wake up at the top of the well, above ground. And, like a dream, I will not be sure how I got out—anymore than I know how I got there. All I know is that I've been there before and gotten out before, and that is the string that winds itself into the rope that at least allows me to hang on until the mysterious thing shows up to pull me out.

Like this mental condition, I'm determined to overcome whatever physical malady has visited me. I just need a walk and an adventure to take my mind off it. I have breakfast in the hotel in the morning, swallowing more cold medicine and an extra cup of coffee. I'm becoming less the cautious newcomer I was when I landed in Delhi. So when I leave the hotel this time, I have only one agenda, to find a way to get lost.

I decide to ease into the day with a Hindi movie, my first. The theatre I go to is billed as the biggest in Rajasthan. Turns out, this isn't saying much. But it's not short on charm, either. The whole affair is an entirely different experience than what we get in the States (which is why you want to travel), from the size of the theatre (not exactly the high-ceiling experience we're used to, but more of a high school classroom), to the seats (not cushy, rocky things, but more like static, stadium seats). Even the screen looks more suited for a junior high auditorium. One of the most memorable surprises, however, is the popcorn, which is sold in little plastic sandwich baggies, like those your mom put in your lunch.

The movie itself is predictably incomprehensible, given the language barrier. A lot of beautiful, apparently ludicrously wealthy, light-skinned Indians dance and sing and move from one exotic location to the next without reason or explanation. There is an intermission. Then, when you come back and are enjoying another tiny bag of homemade popcorn, something terribly sad happens. Like one of the main characters has to go off to work or sell one of his three mansions or something. And there is a great deal of mourning. And his mother apparently feels like she has utterly failed him. But in the end, a long-lost relative shows up and he must be even more rich or something, and probably gives the family another mansion or fancy hotel. And everyone dances again. And things are shiny and happy once more. At least this is what it looks like to my untrained eyes and ears.

Even though I haven't seen that much of India yet, I am suspicious of where these movies are shot, because nothing I've seen yet looks anything remotely like the lush, well-appointed locations in this movie. At least there is no smoking in the theatre, so I am able to sit in clean air for a couple of hours and give my lungs a break.

*   *   *   *

I hear about a monkey temple in the hills just outside the city that is built around a fresh water spring. I'm in no shape to walk there, but I'd love to get away from the crowds for the rest of the day. I decide to hire a rickshaw, even though I've heard stories of backpackers being left there if the rickshaw driver gets a better offer.

I have to ask a surprising number of drivers before one smilingly agrees to the journey. We set the round-trip price, including an hour wait while I walk around. On the short drive there, the driver is curious about why I want to go to the monkey temple. I tell him, mostly I want to get out of the city, but I could also stand a dose of holy water. He asks if I know the story of the temple. *Not really*, I say.

According to the driver, a saint once spent his whole life here, praying for 100 years in this same spot. Before he died, the gods, pleased with his remarkable penance, blessed this spot with abundant water. He says there are 7 natural pools on the temple grounds and the main one is said to never run out of water.

That's a good story, I say.

I will take you to the sun temple first, he says, *it is on the way*.

The drive into the lush Aravalli hills is worth the trip all by itself. We pass two groups of women in colorful saris, a sadu in a bright orange lunghi, a wandering foursome of holy cows, and a playful band of children near the sun temple, who were taking turns pretending to be priests and asking for baksheesh.

Just off to the left, inside the main entrance to the temple grounds, there is a snake charmer wearing a red turban and playing whatever you call that flute with the bulb in the middle. His cobra dances out of a woven basket sitting in front of him. This is the kind of scene I'm not sure what to do with. On a small scale, it's the same thing as the Taj Mahal. I've seen so many depictions of snake charmers, it almost feels like a cliché. But yet, there's an actual dangerous snake sitting within easy striking distance of this man as he casually serenades it. There are not many people here today and the rickshaw driver has elected to walk around with me to tell me more stories. I stop to watch the snake charmer. The rickshaw driver patiently waits for a minute, then he says in my ear, *the poison it's removed, yes.*

What? I answer. *How do you know?*

They are not making money enough to be every day risking death like this.

So it's not the whole music calms the savage beast *kind of thing?*

Cobras are not hearing music the way you and I enjoy. Also, the snake may be taking the doses of bhang, for calming.

Bhang?

Cannabis you are calling it.

Man, what else is not real here? Next you're going to tell me Indians eat cows.

He just looks at me for a long time. Then he finally says, *Some of the cows are not for the eating.*

We tour the different temple structures, including several of the pools, each with its own "priest." The rickshaw driver waves off a couple of advances from these keepers. This is called the monkey

PAINTED OXEN | 89

temple not because it was built as a shrine to the primates, but because it is swarming with the extended clans of two kinds of monkeys. And they are quite used to people. One actually has his hand in my shoulder bag before I see him, but my driver runs him off effortlessly. I snap the bag closed and pull it around in front of me. But the monkeys remain curious and close by.

When we get to the main pool, a place much larger than I anticipated, I tell my guide I'd like to put my feet in the water. He says, *You will be talking to him about the bathing*, pointing to the priest. I approach the priest sheepishly, offering a 10 rupee bill. Surprisingly, the priest holds up his left hand to stop me, and gestures for me to remove my sandals. I do, and with his right hand he swiftly applies a bit of chalky red powder to the middle of my forehead. Then he picks up a smoldering bundle of herbs and blows on it to get the smoke going. He gently blows some smoke in my face, then swirls it above my head. Afterwards, he bows slightly. The rickshaw driver, watching from a few steps up, says, *You are paying him now*. I retrieve the bill, bowing and handing it to him at the same time. Then he opens his hands towards the water and I walk down a number of stairs and into the pool, about mid-calf deep. No one else is in the pool right now, so I have no social cues to follow. The water is surprisingly cool and also invigorating. Maybe it is holy water after all. I reach down with my hands and splash a little on my face, but in my awkwardness, I neglected to take off my shoulder bag, so I have to be careful. I push it around to my back and I am able to bend down into the water more easily. I stay in the water for another minute or so, splashing water on my face and over my head, and feeling its cool silkiness on my legs. Then, because I can think of nothing else to do, I slowly ascend the steps again and rejoin the driver.

When we climb all the way out of the pool's basin, the sun is beginning to set, giving us another show of color. As the sun begins to fade beneath the horizon, we make our way back to the rickshaw. Before we leave, I crouch down on one knee and reach into my bag for a package of biscuits. I cup one in my left hand and place another on the open palm of my right, holding it out to a nearby monkey. He rushes over and quickly snatches it from my hand. My driver gives me a frown. But I am too delighted by the bolt of electricity I feel from that brief contact with a wild being to be ashamed. My face breaks into a big smile, which makes even my driver give up his frown to laugh, and then I hold a second one out for the monkey. I hold this one a little tighter between my thumb and forefinger this time, and the electric connection when it is snatched is drawn out just a little longer. This feeling is addicting, but I know I've pushed it as far as I can with my driver, who would like to get back to town before sundown, and so I stand up and join him once more. As we walk back to the rickshaw, I can still feel the monkey's energy pulsing in my hand.

Once inside my room, I collapse in my bed again. When I wake a couple of hours later, I try to pull myself up to join the others for dinner on the rooftop. But I don't even make it to the stairs. I'm too weak from my day's adventure and I can't stop sneezing. I retreat back to my room and sleep comes almost before I hit the bed.

LA MORT

NUMBER THIRTEEN IN THE MAJOR ARCANA is La Mort, or Death. A skeleton carries a great scythe in the shape of the crescent moon and rides upon a white horse, cutting down all manner of things growing from the earth, including heads, hands, and feet. A rainbow graces the sky behind the skeleton's head.

The moon points the way to renewal, the answer to Death's eternal riddle. Death is the universal absolute. In the eyes of Death all are equal, Kings, Queens, servants, and thieves. Death is the foundation of all creation and the ultimate illusion. One who understands the marriage of creation and destruction has mastered the most fundamental aspects of the divine universe.

–THE BOOK OF MYSTERIES

SCYLLA

LONG AGO THEY CEASED BEING HUMAN. They chose the certainty of devolution over the chance of transcendence, the saltiness of blood over the sweetness of figs. Whatever their reasons, tangible is their hunger.

From his hiding place in the forest, he hears their many legs, even as they appear to float above the ground. He watches silently as their frenetic arms gather and destroy. Their first order is to obey their hunger. Above all else. This obedience binds them to their deepest sorrow, which is that though they consume, they are still hollow. With each cannibalistic act, their ravenous pulse grows stronger. And fulfillment moves farther away.

To reach the bridge, the monk must pass through their world. There is no other way. For a time, he must co-exist with them. If he falls into fear, they will know. And the journey will end here. He will be consumed by their hunger.

To reach the bridge, he must transcend fear. He must overcome the force that rules their existence. To transcend his fear, he must acknowledge it. Examine the lines of its face. Only then can he move through it. Only then will he be intimate enough with it that it will reveal its illusion to him.

To pass through here, he must answer his master's riddle, *What is it to be human?* The answer, he knows, depends upon the test before him. *To be human is to be whole, but to fail to see this wholeness.* In this, they are human. And their hunger is part of everyone.

To pass through here, he must find the stillpoint of wholeness. He concentrates. He becomes still. Self-contained. Motionless but alert. Like a watchful cobra. A hidden lion ready to pounce. He corrals his breath into a narrow and invisible stream. All his thoughts are condensed to the size of a rice grain and hidden in his heart's center, in the secret chamber, the place reserved for great mysteries.

He has opened his heart to better understand this place and its inhabitants, those who know what the earth knows, who live deep in the shadow and entangled in decay. He has trained his mind to imagine their fury, those who long ago traded the secret of fire for the taste of marrow.

The masters who have gone before him, who years earlier marked this trail he now travels, wrote of their dharma on this path. Many times he has read their words, studied their warnings, their accounts of danger, their explanations of the elementals woven into this murky world. He remembers their descriptions of beings who hear what the trees hear and smell what the wind smells, those who swallow the hearts of lizards to harness the dragons in their dreams.

Forget how to blink, he tells his eyes. He becomes the gnarled oak beside him. He breathes through his skin. He knows that if he holds this way of being too long, he may become something else entirely. His feet may sprout roots, and his arms may join the vines whose life's purpose it is to escape their birthplace and ascend to some higher, brighter existence.

He listens. His eyes become ears. His ears become a thousand eyes.

Around him, the rain falls, the fog thickens, and the sounds of the forest invade every crevice of the world. The sensory offerings are intoxicating. They send invitations to climb, to swim, to dance, and to sing. But he resists their temptation.

Time stands motionless, spans the reach of eternity. The fog continues its endless wander. It throws its veils over the world, lifting them, dragging them along behind. In between, he catches glimpses of the ones who have come before. Their bones hang from branches. Their flags, like the words they once spoke, have worn too thin with age to be heard. They were not able to transcend their fears. They were not able to look their monsters in the face. They did not understand the wholeness of all things.

Disappearing into the invisible oneness of this stillpoint, he is free to move again through the external world. He carries this fierce stillness in his heart. He has become it.

PRAEDA

You awake to the sound of a coin landing in a bowl. You are sitting on a purple and gold carpet, pillows under your knees, wrapped in layers of olive colored linen, faded and worn at the edges. The bowl sits in front of you, a few silver coins rest in the bottom. The pipe sits to your left, the mouthpiece still in your hand. An old man with a kind, round face kneels before you. You are a storyteller. And he would like you to tell him a story.

The pipe brought you a new dream of the lions just now. And you decide you will share a page of their story with him.

*   *   *   *

The younger lion, Aragon, remains restless, distrustful. He wants to know what his elder can teach him. He wants the older lion to give him a good reason to stay, to convince him that this is his path, the thing he's been searching for through all this time wandering alone. He wants to know he was right to leave the pride, wants validation for the voice inside him, which has led him so far astray. But he will not say these things.

A long time ago, Mahatru began, *a restless lion stared across the horizon at the meadow before him and the mountains framing it, all illuminated in the moonlight. He could no longer bury his questions inside him.*

*And so he left his pride and traveled across a great river. He aban-
doned his respected and resilient family. Abandoned the certainty of
his future noble position in the pride. He let go of life as he knew it.
And he set himself upon the world to be burned or dazzled by its fires.
He really didn't care which.*

*Unhinged, he wandered. He discovered new terrain. He tested his
mettle against the elements and against the other warriors he encoun-
tered. Without the lionesses of Kali, he had to stalk and kill his own food.
And so he also discovered hunger. He lived close to death at times and
became its intimate. And this intimacy caused him to hone his senses.*

*He called out to the winds at sunset. He grew into the gifts be-
stowed upon him by the moon goddess. Gifts of sight and ear. Gifts
of movement and speed. Gifts of knowledge and understanding. And
after some time, he met another wandering king. Equal to him in size,
color, and mane, gazing upon this other was like looking at himself in
the water's reflection, right down to the moonlight shining in his eyes.*

*Lions have a social order, which must be established immediately
whenever they meet. And which often results in bloodshed, sometimes
death. The two kings did not yet know the full breath of their powers,
let alone their destiny. But something whispered to them. Something
told them they were part of something different, a new way, a new
order. Instead of dueling for a position, for bragging rights, for some
imagined hierarchy, they simply stood for a long time taking each other in. And one-by-one they each let out a series of mighty roars. When
they finished, they walked to a place nearby, under a mango tree that
looked out over a fertile valley. There they lay down side by side under
the full moon.*

*   *   *   *

The old man with the round face bows, thanks you, and takes his
leave.

CHARYBDIS

PUSHKAR. Born of lotus petals, home of camel races. It turns out the races have already been run and I missed them. Just last week, while I was getting sick in Jaipur, hundreds of people converged on this tiny town to race camels and to watch them being raced. I am disappointed I missed this eccentric desert tradition, but it is just as well, because now the town is quiet, uncrowded, and the air is clean. I try to heal myself by running Chi through my chakras, like my friend Sehnka taught me to do in Vienna, but it offers no noticeable cure. I'm not quite bed-ridden. But I cough almost perpetually and move a lot slower than normal. And I don't have much energy. But I am still restless. Which makes my condition that much more intolerable.

Pushkar is another of India's holy cities, with ghats and temples and holy men of more and less reputable pedigrees. I visit the ghats, which consist of many steps leading into a body of water, often a river, like the Ganges, where people either bathe for purification, or are cremated when they die. In this case, the body of water is Lake Pushkar. According to Hindu legend, the lake was created when Brahma dropped petals from a lotus flower to the Earth in this valley.

Like the monkey temple, there are holy men who perform rituals at these ghats. They ask how much I want to offer *to Brahma* in exchange for their services. This is also known as *baksheesh*,

98

which may take the form of a tip or a bribe, depending on the kind of situation you're in. I'm okay with that. But the priest I meet here skips the formalities of actually offering any services and simply demands baksheesh from me just for standing on the steps of the ghats. My cynicism meter moves farther to the right.

At the top of a nearby hill, at the end of a very steep climb, sits the Saraswati temple, named after and dedicated to Brahma's wife of the same name. Still hoping I can beat the chest cold and looking for fresh inspiration, against all better wisdom, I set out to climb it. Steadily, deliberately, and not in any record time, I make it. When, after great effort, I get to the top, I find the temple closed.

I am crestfallen. I turn away from the locked door and stare out across the playa, at the little crescent village on the shores of what I realize from this perspective is really more of a pond than a lake. But taking in the full view from up here, disappointment soon turns to awe, and I begin to feel like I'm a long way away from me. Like I am living someone else's adventure. For the first time, Pushkar feels like a holy place. A place where magic may exist after all. I have faith in India once more, and in my reason for being here. I sit down and stare out across the valley. The sun is approaching the horizon. I did not think to bring my headlamp with me, and I really should be going. But I want to stay. I sit still a little while longer and even meditate on the stone steps. When I open my eyes, the sun is more than halfway hidden behind the small city skyline and I have to scramble down in the fading light before I am trapped out here in the dark.

*   *   *   *

I like being out here. I like that people are, for the most part, at their best. They are open and alive. Conversation is not small or dull. We seem to be able to skip the pleasantries of *how's your day* and get right into the meat of things. Maybe all travel opens us up like this. Or maybe it's just that you don't go to India, at least not to a tiny town in the middle of Rajasthan, unless you are a little interesting to begin with, unless your story has some pages to it.

At dinner, after my climb, I meet an older Jewish man from New York—with a heavy British accent—who is reading a book by Gita Mehta. He sees me from a nearby table with my worn paperback of *The Razor's Edge* turned back on itself in my hands and he digs into his bag to hold up a tattered copy of the same. I move over to his table and our introduction turns into a two-hour discussion of the search for God in literature. He is, I think, too cynical, but we hit it off. He argues, *If I were to meet God, what would I ask him? And what would he really be able to tell me about life and its meaning? Find the answers inside? Here's the meaning of life, as far as I can tell: Pleasure.*

His wife of seventeen years died of complications from pneumonia after a long battle with cancer. For some time afterwards he could find no meaning whatsoever in life. He wasn't even sure why he kept on living. He had other family, and friends, and work, but death had blacked out most of the windows in his life, so that he could not see the light from these things, nor find any comfort in their company. He spent a lot of time alone, walking through Central Park, going to movies, re-reading books, staring at walls. He has only recently taken a lover. And that has brought the only measure of joy back to his life that he has known in years.

When he was much younger, he and a friend spent a month riding trains in India. They had very little money, but the second-class fares were cheap, and they could sleep on the trains. The adventure, and all of its discoveries, from exotic places and foods, to new friends, to conversations that lasted for whole days, was one of the best experiences of his life. He felt more alive during those weeks than he could remember before or after. He booked this trip in an effort to find some trace of that feeling again.

I spend a few more days here in Pushkar, in conversation with my new friend and taking long naps. It happens that British Jewish New Yorker has a car and a driver, and he offers me a ride to Udaipur, where I was planning to go anyway when I felt better. But I'm not getting better. So I opt for a change of scenery instead. The car is also an Ambassador, like the one we rode in to Agra, but it must be a newer version, because it's more comfortable and goes a bit faster. It is a relief to be in a car, with suspension, on a road without four thousand other vehicles. The pollution is almost non-existent out here in the middle of the desert. That and the open landscape allow me to breathe.

*   *   *   *

Death brings out different things in different people. One of those things is the involuntary gawk response. On the way to Udaipur, on a particularly desolate stretch of road, a very unusual gathering catches our attention. And it won't let go. My friend asks his driver to pull over. On the ground is a large animal, a water buffalo perhaps, or what used to be one. Feasting on the carcass are canine predators of various sizes, wild dogs mostly. Sitting in apparent judgment of the dogs (and perhaps the now-departed beast) are rows of vultures, three feet tall, arranged in large semi circles around the event. They look, with their dark coloring, like a black-robed tribunal of death. Or maybe that is a stereotypical vulture prejudice leaking through and they are actually guarding the soul of the beast until it can be transported safely to the other side.

L'AMOUREUX

NUMBER SIX IN THE MAJOR ARCANA is L'Amoureux, the Lovers. A young man is flanked by two beautiful maidens. On his left, a woman in white robes wearing a crown of gold. On his right, a Dionysian priestess, half clothed in velvet and draped in wreaths of grape vines. Cupid is in the corner above him, poised with an arrow he has dipped in a special potion designed to create the illusion of fate.

Two perspectives are possible. The first is straightforward, that the youth stands at a crossroads of free will, where he must choose between virtue and vice. The second, more subtle, is that these two energies are inherent in life, and he must learn to balance the two. In other words, in this life one must neglect neither the spiritual nor the sensual, neither the eternal nor the temporal. This is the beginning of wisdom.

–THE BOOK OF MYSTERIES

SCYLLA

THE RIVER IS BOTH CONSTANT AND MERCURIAL. In all things, the monk relies on her. The river is passionate, wise, knowing, ancient. She is his guide, his companion, his sustenance. She quenches his thirst. She brings him fresh supper, fish, fruits, and foliage. She gives him the shelter of her trees. She is his invisible cloak, his eyes in the dark. Her fierceness protects him from those who will not cross her. And her mighty voice drowns out his clumsiness. She is divine mercy.

The river travels between the border of two worlds, between the Dorje and her lover. Together they create the sacred space here. Each pressing into the other with unyielding desire, with unimaginable patience. As she opens to her lover, her breasts swell into mountains that form the roof of the world. Her sex unfolds into a deep and invisible gorge that disappears between the two worlds. The clouds, observing their union, respond in gushes of rainfall, and the earth shutters and shakes in return. In between, the river flows in and out of their union.

The monk, too, is caught in their terrestrial lovemaking. Just as the Dorje is caught in his. Because, in addition to all else she is to him, and in spite of his vows, the river is also his lover. She seduces him with her song. She guides him gently into her secret places. She tends to his every need. She is divine grace.

The river is the life force of the Dorje, but she is also his life force. Just as he is hers. Just as he is part of everything here. The rocks and the trees. The steep ledges and the mud. The leeches and the biting insects. The snakes he avoids and the fish he eats. He is the rain that falls from the sky and the streams that plunge from cliff walls.

There is little else to be said. There is little else to know. As his master reminds him, *The most essential teachings have never been written down.*

PRAEDA

You awake to the sound of rain gently falling on the thatched roof over your head. You are nuzzled deep under linen sheets. In a pillow-soft bed, with faded curtains blowing near open windows. And grains of sand scattered on worn wooden floors.

In your half sleep, you feel yourself suspended in a moment of perfect peace. Your mind flows freely, like the wind through the curtains. You hear the ocean, rhythmically advancing then retreating. You hear your own breath, gently expanding and contracting.

You turn onto your back, lift your arms above your head and stretch. A rusted fan turns lazily before the backdrop of whitewashed ceiling beams. You open your lungs and breathe in the scent of rain.

You close your eyes and pull up the sheet again. You start to roll onto your other side, and as you turn, your body slides up against another. Naked and smooth. And you realize the rhythmic sound of breathing you hear is not your own.

You lift the sheet, just a little. Looking to let in only enough light to illuminate the mystery. And nothing more. You don't want to break the magic spell. Her long crimson hair, still damp from carrying the ocean in its curls, flows down from her pillow and onto the bed, creating a bridge to your body. Her porcelain skin glows radiant in the half-light. You delicately trace the curve of her back, resting your hand on her hip, and curling up next to her. Your breath falls into rhythm with hers as you drift between the worlds.

CHARYBDIS

The British Big Apple and I have made it to Udaipur, the Venice of the East. For my birthday, I'm treating myself to a nice room in a place with a view, over the water. It sets me back an unthinkable price tag for most backpackers, about $14 a night. And though it isn't quite like giving up on authenticity and checking into an American hotel, it's also probably not the place I'm going to meet a guru. Right now though, I'm still too sick to care about the traveler credo. The best I can do is to sit in this rooftop café, drink ginger tea, and read. Being sick at home is bad enough. Being sick on the other side of the world is like being cold without a coat.

I venture out to a museum with the Big Apple, but I am too light-headed and feverish to stand long enough to make it all the way through. I end up coming back to this cafe, and, in my depleted and near-hallucinatory state, just watching the bats fly overhead, dipping into the water, zooming and twisting and banking at the speed of light. It is a little like being suspended between waking and dreaming.

There is a little mini-mini-market stand near the entrance to the hotel. I collapse into a coughing fit as I am walking by its shopkeepers while coming back from the museum. One of them, a slight, short man with a large grin, puts me on the back of his motorcycle and takes me to what looks like an abandoned school that is now a medical clinic, where I stand in line for most of the morning. The payoff is well worth it though, an Indian doctor, trained in the States, who examines me, asks me questions in English, and gives me a scrip for four meds. Then the guy on the motorcycle drives me to a pharmacy on the side of the road, which is about the size of a chai stall, where I find out you don't even need a scrip, if you know what to ask for. And the price for everything is less than a night's stay at my hotel.

The meds start working almost immediately. And by evening, five of us go to dinner at the Lake Palace for my birthday. We take a boat to the hotel, which at first glance comes off as sort of a rhinestone version of luxury. It's all sparkles and shines, and a little over-done, glamorous in a 70's James Bond kind of way. We sit on white leather couches in an open bar, with high-ceilings and crystal chandeliers, and have overpriced and unmistakably bad champagne. But it is still champagne, in a land that appears to be entirely barren of anything resembling bottled fermented grapes. The champagne is followed by a lavish and delicious vegetarian buffet. But the most important thing is that it's the first night I haven't coughed all the way through dinner.

*   *   *   *

In the morning, New York and I meet an Egyptian girl at breakfast in the upstairs café and invite her to our table. Breakfast is polite, but short. We're all headed to different places for the day, but agree to meet up for dinner. I'm finally feeling better and need to cure a serious case of cabin fever.

Religion takes up most of the pages in history, it seems. Theocracies, crusades, and wars of all stripes and sizes. Borders, languages, and beatitudes all shaped by religion. Turns out, religion steals a fair amount of the traveler's attention, as well. Temples, cathedrals, and mosques dominate much of the architecture wherever you take yourself on the planet. Mostly with good cause. In India, it's architecture worth seeing. So I take a rickshaw to the City Palace and ask directions to the Jagdish Temple.

The Jagdish is dedicated to the deity Vishnu, the dreamer and preserver of the Universe. Spanning three stories, it is the largest temple in Udaipur. I climb an imposing set of stairs leading up to the temple itself. Then I must go through a couple of outer chambers before I come to the steps that lead to the main shrine, where Lord Vishnu resides. I am looking up at my destination, when an old man appears at the top, peering down at me. This will sound odd, but somehow it feels like he has been waiting there for me. I hesitate for a moment, a little thrown off by his intentional gaze, not knowing whether to continue climbing or to turn and go another direction. I decide to keep climbing, and when I reach him, his intensity is relaxed a bit. He is still looking at me, but his eyes are kind and his presence feels more benevolent than intrusive. I greet him with a *Namaste* and a slight bow, my palms pressed together in front of my heart. He returns the bow and smiles serenely. Then he turns to look at the giant birdlike figure guarding the doorway in front of us. *It is a Garuda.* He says, after a moment. *Part is man and part is eagle. Lord Vishnu's vehicle of first choice.* He adds. *But what almost no one is knowing, is that this is also the very first and most original phoenix.* This last part he says somewhat confidentially, in a quieter voice, spoken with his head tucked down and a little closer to my ear.

We walk past the Garuda and through the great doorway into the main shrine. Inside is a large black statue of a figure with four arms. I only know it is Vishnu because of its billing in the guidebook. Without some kind of clue, I don't know Vishnu from

Shiva from Krishna. Well, I guess Krishna is usually painted blue. So that's kind of a giveaway. And there's also Ganesh, I think there's only one elephant-headed deity. But show me a brass or stone statue of any other Hindu deity and I'll generally just have to guess.

Being made completely of a single piece of stone. He tells me, proudly, as if he carved it himself. It is symbolizing the unities of all things. Everything in this temple is teaching about unity. This chamber of Vishnu is being surrounded by four others, one is for the Sun God, another is the Goddess Shakti, next is Lord Shiva, and the last one is being the wonderful Lord Ganesha. All Hindu temples are being built in this way. The why is because these are the places where the divine and the human freely are living together. As you are seeing, there are no gates in here. No doors are separating the human world from the worlds of these deities. This is having an intentional purpose. This is because Indians are knowing that separation is folly thinking. The world is not separate things. Everything is existing at once, in the same places, with you and me, just now.

I stare for a while at the giant black stone statue of Vishnu, trying to take in what the old man is telling me. I watch the others here, almost all of whom are Indians, come and bow and offer their gifts to the Lord of the Universe. I wonder if they understand, the way my spontaneous and benevolent guide does, the simple beauty of this symbol. After a minute, I turn to ask him a question about the meaning of the black stone, but he is no longer there. Instead, to my right, where he was, a sadhu sits, a single orange cloth around his waist, his hair wrapped up on top of his head, his eyes closed. I look around, but the old man is nowhere to be found. And I think that maybe I'm dreaming again. I pinch my arm. It hurts. But I'm not sure this is an accurate test. Who decided that was a thing, anyway?

Back at the hotel, over dinner, Egypt, New York, and I talk about all the things you're ideal dinner companions would want to discuss: books, movies, history, travel, and geographic culture. But also the things travelers, who barely know each other, are able to talk about more freely than others. You know, the four taboos: religion, politics, money, and even sex. The last of which, Egypt is the one to bring up. Albeit, subtly. We are discussing our experiences of India, and she explains she's just finished a month-long Tantra yoga workshop. She's been seeking a teacher for some time, back in London, but just decided to make a vacation out of it. She figures at least in India she might be able to have a more authentic experience. She might even find a teacher with a legitimate lineage in the art. Then she quickens the topic a bit, admitting she is not just seeking enlightenment, but also better sex. Following this, out it tumbles that she doesn't think she's had really good sex. But then she backpedals a little, maybe to brush off the looks of something close to pity she gets from us. She says, quickly, looking down at the table, *well, I mean I've had good sex, but not, you know, mind-blowing sex.* Then she looks back up, at me. Only for an instant, but it's effective. I'm not sure New York catches it. But I do.

Suddenly my whole world changes. That's all it takes sometimes. A subtle glance. A few words casually strung together and uttered softly. We try and we pine and we plan and we coordinate and we want and we need. We write poems and read books. We pay for nice dinners and lingerie. We buy flowers. We send messages. And God, how we flirt. And then, just like that, there it is. And we didn't have to do a damn thing except be ourselves. And do what we were already doing. And love, or at least something like it, just comes and sits in front of us and tells us it would really, really like to have mind-blowing sex. So much so that it has come all the way to India looking for it.

I play it as cool as I can. We finish diner, wrap up our conversation, and each say goodnight. She excuses herself first, which gives New York and I the opportunity to take verbal note of the invisible room key she may have laid on the table. He says he's too old for her. And I confess, though I'm feeling much better, my day trip took a lot out of me, and I'm definitely not back to 100%. Not close enough to 100% to provide mind-blowing sex, anyway.

Back in my room, though, I seriously rethink it. Actually, I do more than that. Since she also mentioned that her room was cold, I gather up an extra blanket from my bed and walk downstairs, through a large courtyard, down a hallway and over to her room, blanket in hand. I stand outside her door for something short of a small eternity, but I can't muster the courage to knock. I start to walk away, then turn back again. I give myself the *isn't-this-what-you-came-here-for* speech and resolve to just leap. With my knuckles in the air and poised at her door, the sudden urge to cough returns without warning. I retreat a few steps away as quickly as I can and muffle my cough into the blanket. I look back at her door, as if I could tell by looking at it whether she heard me. I hesitate a few more seconds then take the coughing as divine intervention and retreat quickly and cowardly to my room.

Egypt is not at breakfast in the morning. I ask at the front desk and they tell me she checked out first thing this morning, to catch an early train.

L'IMPÉRATRICE

NUMBER THREE IN THE MAJOR ARCANA is called *L'Impératrice*, the Empress. A luminous winged woman sits upon a throne. She is pregnant. In her left hand she holds a scepter, on her right arm a flaming phoenix appears about to take flight.

She sits amidst a vast and fertile field of grains. Her head is crowned with a halo of twelve stars. Her left foot is cradled by a crescent moon. Her right foot is encircled by a serpent. All initiates are reborn into the material world from the womb the mother of the three-fold spiritual world.

–THE BOOK OF MYSTERIES

SCYLLA

His journey is not a reflection of the moon. It is the moon itself. He is not separate from this quest. It is his dharma, his path, his voice. It is not a bead on a mala, not a veil to remove. It is the cooperation of elements, the marriage of spirit and flesh. It is the shadow of faith, the reflection of being. It is the full metaphor. It is all there is.

In order to cross any threshold, it is essential to keep at least one hand on the rock. The rock has known the rain for as long as fire can remember. The rain has caressed its surfaces smooth of the trace of any other lovers. And here and there, the moss has stretched its hand-woven blankets over the rock's breast, for protection. If he can understand this, he will find purchase to traverse any chasm.

If the Dorje is to guide, then he must be willing to follow. If she is to quench his thirst, then he must be willing to bend to meet her. If she is to feed him, then he must be willing to eat. If she is to bathe him, then he must be willing to be naked before her, to enter her without fear or shame. If she is to speak, then he must learn how to listen. If she is to reveal her mysteries, then he must be patient and open.

If, through the swarm of insects and the heat of the threatening sky, he seeks the certainty of breath, then he too must become fluid, etheric. If the heat of body, earth, and sky are unbearable, then he must bend his mind towards the tempest. If the wind is to lift him up, then he must be willing to fly.

If he would eat of the fruits of the earth, then he must have the courage to steal fire. If he would warm his skin, his blood, his bones, then he must master his inner light. If he would know the secrets of the heart, then he must become an alchemist.

PRAEDA

You are walking up a long, winding staircase. The stairs are made of stone, the walls are thick, and the air damp. The only light comes from candles appearing sporadically along the stairwell walls. You walk slowly, as if each step were a prayer, a walking meditation. As if each step had a name, and you whisper it softly with each small ascension. You are climbing towards something, an unknown destination, an imagined horizon, a promise of light. But as you ascend, every step eclipses the larger purpose in some small way.

Along the stairway, you pass several deities. Brahma, Vishnu, Shiva, Krishna, Buddha, Kali. They are each spaced a few hundred steps apart, sitting in small cubbies carved into the wall, candles at their feet. You stop briefly to pay homage to each, to offer a flower or some rice from your pack, to light a candle.

In one cubby is a seated lion. You don't understand what deity it represents. You see a small booklet lying beside the lion and open it. On the first page are only symbols you don't understand. They are Egyptian, maybe, and include a bird, a wavy line you take to indicate water, and a sun disk. You turn a page, and it reads: *House of Horus, Home of the Seven Hathors*, followed by more symbols, including a lion's head. You turn another page, but cannot read any of the symbols written there. You turn several other pages, but the images become even more incomprehensible. You return the booklet and continue walking up the steps.

You pass several more deities, mostly Hindu. Then you see another image that seems out of place, a lion-headed, bare-breasted woman with long hair. On the wall of the cubby behind her, it reads: *Daughter of Ra.* Then, below that, in smaller letters: *Goddess of Love, Ruler of Stormy Skies, Mirror of the Soul.*

You write these names down in your journal, but you're not exactly sure why. You sit with the lion goddess a few moments longer than the others, though you can't explain the why of this either. She is familiar to you somehow. Like you've dreamt of her, seen her in a museum, or studied her in some art class a long time ago.

Eventually, you give up trying to sort it out, and you move on again, up the stairs. When you reach the top, there is a great light. You sit down and rub your hands together, letting your body absorb the heat. You cannot tell where the light comes from, only that it is comforting. After a while, your body warm and your mind rested, you begin your descent. The summit is never the end of the journey.

CHARYBDIS

I AWAKE IN THE SAND DUNES, under the full moon, to the sound of camels slowly munching. Like so often when traveling, I'm disoriented for a moment. *Wait, sand dunes, camels, gigantic moon, I'm dreaming, right?*

Only one sensation offers an answer to that riddle. Before I went to sleep, the camel wallah laid a thick, heavy blanket over me. I can feel its surprising weight on the full length of my body. The blanket is a ballast, grounding me, reminding me I'm resting on the earth and not suspended in the dream world. It acts as an emotional swaddle out here in the middle of nowhere, cut loose from anything remotely familiar.

Lying here, held fast by blanket and bed of sand, I stare up into the heavens in utter amazement. At the dramatic beauty of the blue-black sky that acts as a backdrop for the swollen moon, and—despite the brilliant moonlight—more stars than I've ever seen in my life. Okay, except for that time I did acid in the desert. I am miles from the nearest city and that city is many miles from anything else. This distance gives me space, not just to see the world with more clarity, but to imagine a place for me in it.

*   *   *   *

I have parted company with British New York to travel on my own to the magical city of Jaisalmer, the Golden City, on the edge of this desert land called Rajastan. I venture up into the farthest reaches of the old walled city, to a guest house called Hotel Paradise. At the entrance, a large Indian man in a great turban greets me with a hearty, *Welcome to Paradise*, in a deep, resonant voice that could belong to James Earl Jones.

I rent a room with a view of the rooftops of the walled city and of the long abandoned Summer Palace in the distance. The old fortress is quiet and soothing, its thick, ancient walls a kind of dream barrier to the world outside. After a few dreamy days of wandering the narrow passages and browsing the antiquity shops, though, the even more romantic notion of a camel safari entices me to venture out again. And so I pack a knapsack, stow my backpack at the hotel desk, and set out.

*   *   *   *

Seeing the world from the back of a camel lends a perspective not easily forgotten. The camel drivers provide the campfires, food, and traditional camel wallah songs and stories. Nature takes care of the sweeping vistas and one-of-a-kind sunsets. The scenery of endless sand dunes combined with the contemplative rocking motion of the camels is meditative and gives further respite from the bustle of much of India.

As we sit around the fire finishing our dinner, the main wallah begins to spin his tale. Tonight he chooses the story of the Goddess Mata Tanot, who guards a temple at the border with Pakistan, not too far from here.

Our chief wallah is Muslim and his assistant is Hindu, though their repertoire includes stories not only from Muslim and Hindu culture, but also from Tibetan Buddhist teachings, Chinese folk tales, and Mongolian mythology. Tonight the story involves two wars between India and Pakistan. In 1965 and 1971. During both wars, hundreds of bombs were dropped near the temple of Mana Tanot, where there was a temporary Indian Army outpost. The story goes that because of the protection of the Goddess, not a single bomb hit the temple. Even more strange, many bombs that were falling close to the temple simply did not explode at all. This happened in both wars.

Because of these unexplained events, as a show of respect, the Indian Army has set up a small permanent base out there, and the soldiers and the inhabitants of the temple look after one another. Some of the unexploded bombs have even been collected by the soldiers, dismantled, and placed on display in the temple. Sort of like a shrine to Mana Tanot's great powers of protection.

The camel wallah takes a long pause in his story, during which he stares gently at each of us and smiles with a kind of childlike amusement, then he continues. The wallah says there is very little rainfall in this part of the desert and successful agriculture is rare out here. Wells are sometimes drilled hundreds of feet deep only to run dry. Yet, near this temple of Mana Tanot, there is an oasis. And those who live there are able to grow plenty of food all year long.

When we arrive back in town, it's late in the afternoon on Christmas day. At the desk to retrieve my pack and get resettled in a new room, I'm invited to Christmas dinner in an outdoor restaurant. I sit at a long table with a dozen familiar faces I've been crossing paths with for weeks. There is a five-piece sitar band, all dressed in white linen, sitting cross-legged as they play. There are paper lights strung overhead. And none of it has the feeling of being cheap or contrived. It occurs to me again that I really am on the other side of the world.

* * * *

The next day I walk out to the Summer Palace - past the Indian policemen all carrying their long sticks—and I find a fully intact cow's skull, horns and all, completely picked clean and sun-bleached. Now, in some states in India, primarily due to its sacred status in Hinduism and Jainism, the slaughter of cattle is prohibited. Also, about the time I arrived in India, there were escalated skirmishes between some Hindus and Muslims that involved the slaughter of numerous cows. Aware of the trouble I could be causing myself, and yet unable to resist this rare opportunity, I pick up the skull, wrap the horns with my shawl, put it in my shoulder bag, and walk back into town. In order to get to my guesthouse, I must walk directly past the huddle of policemen and their sticks. I am almost certain I'll be stopped for questioning. There is an instant when I am approaching that one of the officers looks up at me. My heart skips. Now there's no way I can turn around. I have no choice but to keep walking. To my great relief, somehow I make it past the policemen and into the fort without any questions.

In much of India cardboard is not used for mailing. Instead, one takes packages to a tailor who sews the contents up into a kind of fabric container and then seals the sewed seams with wax. I ask around for a tailor inside the old fort and take the skeletal souvenir to him to package it up for mailing. The tailor is nervous about the job, for obvious reasons, and wants me to sign a piece of paper saying he did not package it for me. I try to explain the absurdity of this. Eventually he relents, but not before charging me a premium.

I take the package to the post office, writing on several forms that it is a souvenir, and then wait in the crowded line with my conspicuously large package. The official behind the counter, however, is suspicious and asks me to open it. I protest, explaining that if I open it, then I'll have to go get it sealed again, and then we'll have the same problem. It'll be a never-ending loop. He leaves the counter and goes back to talk to another man, possibly his supervisor. The two men talk for a while and then the man who was helping me goes to help another customer and the supervisor heads my way. I have to explain the exact same thing to the supervisor. He looks at me with a blank slate and then goes back and digs in a file cabinet for another form. Terrified that I'm about to end up in an Indian prison indefinitely, I consider dropping the package right there and bolting from the building. The second man comes back with a two-page form for me to fill out. At that moment words fall from the sky and into my mouth and I tell him I have to be somewhere, but I'll take the form with me, fill it out, and bring it and the package back later. Somehow this works and I manage to leave the post office still in possession of the package and not under arrest.

Panicked, I secret the package-turned heavy yolk back to my room as quickly as possible, and then immediately go to the train station to book passage to Jodhpur for the next morning. I'm thinking that if I mail it in a bigger city, it won't draw as much attention.

The next morning I wake early, dress, pack, grab the bulky yellow (did I mention yellow) parcel, and head out for the train. But before I get there, I chicken out. I start to think about all the ways this little novelty adventure could go bad—including police interrogations and links to the volatile groups who have been slaughtering holy cows of late. Not to mention the trouble of lugging around this conspicuously hard to carry package, on and off trains, and in and out of guesthouses, in addition to my backpack. In a split-second decision, I abandon the parcel in an empty alley, change my destination at the station, and hop the morning train to Gujarat.

LE PENDU

NUMBER TWELVE IN THE MAJOR ARCANA is called *Le Pendu*, the Hanged Man. A young man hangs by his left leg from a horizontal beam, suspended between two sycamore trees. The right leg of the youth is crossed in back of the left and his arms are folded behind his back, forming an inverted symbol of Sulphur, symbolizing the *magnum opus*.

A stuffed bag is tucked under one arm, from which coins fall to the ground.

In order to reach the heights of enlightenment, the world must be turned on its head. That which is base must be elevated, and that which is heady must be subjugated. In this way, gold is transformed from a personal possession into a way of being.

−THE BOOK OF MYSTERIES

SCYLLA

HE CARRIES THE MACHETE ON HIS BACK. A gift from his master. Given to him many years ago when he was first granted refuge. Then, committed to a path of non-violence, he could not understand how he would ever have use for it. Now he knows. It is a compass to find his path through the jungle.

The machete is a fine tool. With it he is able to cut through otherwise impenetrable territory. Though it proves useless against the downpours of rain that come without warning, before he can find shelter. Like the one he is caught in just now. The rain's heavy veils block the rest of the world from view. And the swiftest of wrists cannot cut through its liquid walls.

He is forced to climb upwards, through the day's sudden darkness. Up to the glimpse of rocky outcrop he spies when a strike of lightening briefly pulls back the rain's curtain. The ground ripples in his wake. The earth around him seems to have lost the will to resist the water's flow. His feet have no choice but to follow where it goes. Rocks tumble beside him, behind him, from under his feet. He loses his balance over and over. Falls to one knee and then the other. He pauses in between, laughing quietly. Patiently he gets back up. Keeps climbing.

He continues like this. Up. Down. A little sideways. Up again. Down. And through his frustration, between his hard breaths, he keeps smiling, laughing to himself. Until he reaches a small ledge that opens up a door to a tiny world the rain cannot enter. Here he sits and rests. Closing his eyes. To see the world more clearly.

He is still seeking the bridge. The one that reaches across the river to the hidden falls. To the treasure the ancient Master hid there in another age, to keep it safe until the world was ready for it. Some say the bridge has been destroyed. By an earthquake. Or a landslide. Or some force unknown. But he knows there is more to it than that.

His ears have been trained to the voices of the mystics. They visit him in his dreams. Where they speak the language of the river. Where they tell him the bridge still stands. Still waits for the one who can see. For the one who must not only find a bridge, but become one.

The rain reminds him that one travels to sacred places in order to awaken that which lies sleeping within. He journeys on this path not to escape the world, but to enter it more deeply. Sometimes that is the only way we can open the doors to our own hearts, to realize that the whole of the earth lives inside the human heart.

Under the stillness of the rocky roof, he dreams of his master. They go for a walk down by the river and stand at the edge of the world. As they look down, the river is singing loudly, boiling up in riots of foam and spray. There are fragments of trees, bleached and polished, laying wedged between the giant boulders, holding open their arms to catch the errant sunlight. His master gestures with an open palm.

Though his eyes see no safe passage, he trusts his master's guidance, remembers his words. *You must learn to see what is hidden. You must become the bridge between.* With each step of the journey, with each word spoken, with each small act of faithfulness, a new doorway is opened, and another log falls into place over the chasm.

PRAEDA

ONCE YOU HAVE TAKEN CARE TO PATIENTLY COAX the light to the surface, many things are possible. An alchemist must be able to hold the possibility of color up to the surface of the water, without thrusting it out into the air, where it will die of overexposure.

An alchemist, like a lover, must know how to hold the beloved safely near the falls of ecstasy, without plunging over the cliff too soon. To be able to rest in this heightened state, in order to enjoy all the brilliant colors of the dawn. The darkness is lush and sensual, and the day is bright and bold, but there is nothing like the in-between world of dawn to show us the full spectrum of beauty's awakening.

If you can hold this image, the peacock will awaken and come out to spread its tail. The rush of colors will come suddenly and brilliantly. All the layers of the rainbow, in shining iridescence, will splash across your lover's face and the two of you will travel through breathless dimensions in the space of a heartbeat.

This is the bridge to the other side. You must beware, though. To the uninitiated, these magnificent effects may trick you into believing you've arrived at the gates of heaven. It is not so. For the dawn is neither the end nor the beginning. It is a midpoint on a circle. The peacock signals the traveler that he is on the right path. That he has crossed the mighty river. That he has witnessed the Gryphon taking flight. But you must continue to follow its flight, eventually the Gryphon will drop its magical tail feathers along your path to guide you.

CHARYBDIS

THOUGH I DON'T LIKE TO TRAVEL WITH AN ITINERARY, or even much of a plan, for reasons I will explain, there are a few places I set out to visit in India. The first is Dharamsala, home of the Dalai Lama. The second, Ghandi's Ashram. Third is to catch a glimpse of one of the few remaining Asiatic lions left on the planet at the Sasan Gir Lion Sanctuary. And the fourth is Sai Baba, a mysterious holy man who lives in Southern India.

I kind of missed the first target, as I went South from Delhi and not North. Though I lied to myself for a while, I am now mostly resigned to the idea that I probably won't make it back up to Dharamsala, as momentum now pushes me in a different direction. The slight regret in the path I've chosen is assuaged a little by the fact that it is very cold in Dharamsala right now. And though I'm curious as to why Tibetans would need to escape the winter, I'm told His Holiness and his entourage often winter in the Southern town of Mysore. I take consolation in the fact that my chosen path may lead to their winter home after all.

I'm forced to admit I'm not really that hearty a person. Though I sleep in backpacker rooms and eat backpacker food and travel second-class rail and ride on Krishna buses and eat in local food stalls and sometimes carry my backpack a respectable distance, I'm not really one of them. I'm afraid sooner or later they'll figure this out. There are several telltale signs: I always get my own room

- no sleeping on roofs or in backpacker dorms; usually my room has a bathroom in it—cause it's just not that much more money; and I can't roll hash to save my life—or smoke much of it. So far though no one seems to hold these things against me.

Despite these limits, somehow I have managed to navigate my way to Ahmedabad, in the state of Gujarat, where Gandhi set up his ashram way back in 1915. By tomorrow, I'll be able to check at least one thing off my list. Not that checking things off the list is the point, really. Not that I am completely sure of the point, either, as you know by now. There is the experience and also the need to feel like I've accomplished something, but I can't say that either tops the fulfillment charts. I suppose I'm hoping that being here will change me somehow. That I'll be able to soak up an insight, an intention, a vibration. That walking this corner of the Earth, it will raise my spirits, open my worldview, relieve my doubts. Is it too naïve to think that salvation might be waiting for me in Gandhi's hometown? Probably. But can you think of a better place to look?

Just like at the Taj, I walk barefoot around the Sabarmati Ashram. I visit the small quarters where Gandhi lived, slept, and I guess occasionally ate—though in most pictures you see it always seems like it's been a while since he's had a meal. At the Ashram today they are still engaged in the art of spinning fabric, as inspired by Gandhi, including making the spinning wheels themselves. They also continue the art of paper-making and other handicrafts.

I read quotes from Gandhi posted on plaques around the ashram, sit on the same floor where he meditated, and try to absorb the essence of this place. It is inspiring, true, though I feel like a bit of a fraud just being here. Who am I to sit on Gandhi's ground? Gandhi walked a thousand miles barefoot. Sure it took me a few planes, trains, and buses to get here, but then all I did to get here was walk across a bridge that bears his name, with shoes on.

I take some pictures, scribble some notes, and try to remind myself just how epic a traveler's trophy this is. But I'm not feeling it. Instead, everything feels a little flat. I feel like a tourist. If Gandhi were here, and he'd even bother to talk to me, he'd probably shake his head and ask me what I thought I was doing. He'd probably gently scold me and tell me that *one does not become spiritually evolved simply by filling a Spiritual Places Passport with stamps.*

The visit to Sabarmati leaves me feeling inadequate in ways I hadn't anticipated. I'm used to being an underachiever. I'm okay with it. In fact, I like being an underachiever. It means something more than just drinking too much wine and reading too much poetry. It means I haven't blindly bought in to someone else's version of what to do with a life. I have purposely stayed still, gone slow, thought about things, considered reasons, purposes, history, chance. In my own way, I've lived with intention, contemplation. I am an antonym to the scratching and clawing of the rest of the ever-climbing human race. But what, ultimately, has this meant? In the face of Gandhi's contemplative and purposeful life, it seems ghostly thin.

To clear my head of this chatter, I decide to walk to the Zoo on Kankaria Lake, which is on the other side of town. Using only the small map in my ubiquitous guidebook and a stubborn male determination not to ask directions, I head out on foot, refusing several offers from rickshaw drivers along the way. It is an hour later before I realize I am hopelessly lost. I finally stop at a sugar water stand and ask for directions. Turns out I'm miles off course. After a bit of negotiating, the brother of the sugar water wallah ends up driving me to the zoo for a fair price, but more than I would've had to pay one of those rickshaw drivers an hour ago.

Despite my naïve courage and desire to disappear into local culture, in new cities I'm sometimes a bit hesitant to drink water without a sealed cap. This is a sore spot with both the sugar water wallah and his brother when I, as politely as I can manage, turn down their offer of a sample of their goods. Nevertheless, I get where I want to go.

I stay at the zoo until almost sunset. It's true, zoos can sometimes be depressing. But somehow I'm always drawn to them while traveling. And I always seem to find something there that makes it worthwhile. This time is no different. I sit on benches and watch the different animals for hours, and it helps me to relax. Something in their nature is soothing. I'm reminded of Rilke and his panther. He wrote one of his first celebrated poems in a zoo, just sitting and watching a caged panther. He watched and he watched, and he didn't write a word, until he actually saw the essence of the animal. Only then did he give himself permission to write about it.

I do my best to do this. And while I don't pretend to have Rilke's vision, I sit and I stare at the lions. I wonder why they have invaded my dreams. And I try to picture myself inside the high walls with them. I try to picture myself inside their skin, held up by their bones, feeling what they feel, seeing what they see, opening their huge jaws and roaring their magnificent roars. Wondering how on earth I find myself in this place.

*   *   *   *

Since I'm already on the South end of town, I hire a ride back across the river to an outdoor restaurant called Vishalla. I sit on the ground, cross-legged, with a small drum under each knee. The table is a cross section of a very large banana tree and the plate is an oversized banana leaf. This is no tourist restaurant; it is authentic at its core. But it is still a richer man's version of a thali. Course after course, portion after portion are served on the banana leaf, accompanied by three different kids of roti to scoop up the food. And anytime I am about to finish something, a waiter arrives to offer more. The food might be the best I've had so far in India. Of course, my opinion may be influenced by the romantic environment, the torches and strings of lights, and the charming service. The food is unbelievable, though. The chef has stayed true to traditional roots, while stretching his boundaries far beyond street food. His creations feature complementing layers of subtle and spicy, rich and delicate. Between my visit to the lions and this perfect feast, I'm feeling better. For the moment, at least, I'm okay with not being Gandhi.

LA JUSTICE

NUMBER EIGHT IN THE MAJOR ARCANA is called *La Justice*. In her left hand, Lady Justice holds up a pair of scales, while in her right she wields a sword. She wears a crown, and her throne sits at the top of three steps.

Justice has a long braid of hair, draped like a necklace around her neck and back over her shoulder. She is blindfolded so she will not rely upon that which is visible. She warns that only those who balance Heaven and Earth will pass safely before Osiris and through the Hall of Judgment.

–THE BOOK OF MYSTERIES

SCYLLA

LIKE A MOUNTAIN GOAT, he traverses the small rocky ledges of the great canyon. The river has fallen far below him here, though he can still hear her voice. It is not the voice of a siren, leading him to his demise. But a gentle reminder of her kept promise to him over these rugged days and weeks.

How does one walk the thin ledge of a thousand-foot-deep canyon, he wonders. The answer comes silently. *The same way one crosses over rocks in a small stream or over a fallen tree. There is only the next step. And then the next.* And her voice to soothe him. There is nothing else.

Thousands of years she has roamed this canyon. She knows every depth and every eddy, every facet of every stone. She has carved her initials into its long face over and over. She has smoothed its jagged edges again and again. Always the rock gives in to her desires. It has no choice.

He knows that to succeed he must learn her secrets. In a way, he must become her. He must flow as gracefully along her high walls as she does below, always subtly bending the rock to his will.

He must not rely upon sight alone. The eyes play tricks up here. And they are in conspiracy with the mind. *All mastery is about doing that which the senses tell us cannot be done.*

He must float his way across. He must dream himself to the other side. In dreams we can all fly. There is no falling. There is not even a hard landing. We have much to learn from dreams.

PRAEDA

YOU ARE IN A VINTAGE COURTROOM. Everywhere you look there is oiled wood. An elevated and ornate judge's bench, where an old man with a white wig and a shiny black robe looks out over his fiefdom. A simple witness stand, where a faceless person sits before a chrome microphone. A long jury box, surrounded by a carved rail, and filled with concerned faces and fidgeting bodies. Worn floorboards, faded paneling, and even huge dark beams overhead.

Looking around, you realize you are sitting at one of the counsel tables. A man in a suit standing at the other table is talking to the jury and pausing occasionally to point at you. Eventually it occurs to you that you are not merely an observer here. You are on trial, for crimes unknown.

The prosecutor is making his closing arguments to the jury. He argues that you are guilty of all kinds of vague crimes. Most of the time you can't quite make out his descriptions of your misdeeds. It seems he is recounting the cardinal sins. You catch part of his plea to the jury, *…envy, sloth, lust…* You want to stand up and say something, but you can't think of any defense. You're not even sure what you're defending against. *These acts are the acts of a recidivist. Of one engaged in sustained self-idolatry.* You hear him say, while you see a few heads in the jury box nod ever so slightly.

You are beginning to despair. The prosecutor deals a final blow and swiftly turns and takes his seat. You become aware of a figure seated next to you at about the same time she rises, walks around the counsel table, and moves towards the jury. She is dressed in a white business suit, with a light blue scarf, her scarlet hair pinned up neatly on her head. She removes the thin black frames from her eyes, folds them in her hands, and ever so sweetly begins to explain to the good people of the jury your virtues. *Hope, compassion, curiosity. Playfulness, courage, generosity...* She considers each juror in turn, holding their individual attention completely, even bringing a tear to the eyes of a few.

When she is finished speaking, she stands for a moment longer, making eye contact with each juror. Then she thanks them for their attention and turns back towards you. When you look up at her, the features of her face are obscured, eclipsed by a great light coming from behind her head. As she walks back towards you, there is a roar of thunder in the distance. Then all the wooden walls and beams of the courtroom fall away. Blue sky shows through gathering clouds that begin to move slowly overhead. Giraffes and elephants stand up from the jury box and a hyena abandons a briefcase at the prosecutor's table and flees what used to be the courtroom.

She stands beside you once more and puts her arm around your shoulder. Then she leans in towards you and tells you in a polished and professional tone, but with what might be a slight smirk, *You're free to go.*

CHARYBDIS

Sensually sated and feeling better about not being someone I am not, someone I perceive to be better at being human than I am, I decide to leave Ahmedabad on a high-note. I depart the next morning for the tiny island of Diu, a former Portuguese colony off the peninsular west coast of India. Because of its size and the fact there's really no traffic to speak of, I decide to rent a scooter and go exploring. The experience of being in traffic is so harrowing in most of India that I usually just take rickshaws or walk. Also, due to the Brits, they drive on the left, which adds just too many points to the hazard scale.

Traveling in India is difficult. Roads are noisy and dangerous and it takes a long time to get anywhere. Whether you're on a train, a bus, or a rickshaw, it is crowded, uncomfortable, smelly, or all three. Maybe that has something to do with why I'm becoming a little cranky, but it's not the only thing. My disenchantment seems to grow a little every day, even though I am trying hard to stave it off with daily gratitude exercises. I mean, look at me. I'm traveling in exotic locations. I've got no real obligations or responsibilities. I'm on a largely forgotten island in the Arabian Sea, riding a scooter in a t-shirt, a lungi, and sandals. The sun is shining, my room is paid for, and the wind is literally in my hair.

Even with all these things to be thankful for, much of the freedom and exhilaration I felt when I landed in the Paharganj has disappeared. I'm not sure where it went. It could be the constant vigilance against scams and pleas for money, or the increasing sense of purposelessness I feel. Whatever it is, I resolve to train my mind to think differently. Maybe my sense of freedom has escaped the mainland, too, and it is somewhere on this island waiting for me. Maybe it came here just so I'd follow it. Maybe it has a plan. I decide the only way to know for sure is to go in search of it.

I drive around a while on my rented scooter until I find a giant fort from the Portuguese days. It's overgrown with grass and weeds, entirely without caretakers, or admission fees, or any protective railings for its open stone stairs, some of which lead to the tops of its fifty feet high walls. I decide there must not be any personal injury lawyers in India. It seems to be a culture steeped in throwing caution to the wind. Everywhere I watch locals ride four to a scooter. Dad drives, small child stands up front between dad's legs, and mom sits side-saddle on the back, holding the baby.

I go inside the fort and start walking around through its overgrown foliage. I climb up its giant steps and walk its high walls, despite the danger that a strong ocean wind could easily topple me into an abrupt, rocky end. I am exploring its former rooms, half walls without ceilings, when I turn a corner to find what looks to be three drunk locals hanging out in a corner. One of them, a big, slovenly looking man, quickly stands up and starts walking over to me, speaking words I can't understand. So far in India, I've been annoyed, scammed, and inconvenienced, but never scared. But as the big, disheveled man rushes in my direction, his wild eyes fixed on me, I start to panic.

I try to remain calm. I just smile and put up my hand in what I hope is a friendly gesture of *Oh, hello. I didn't mean to interrupt. I'll be going back the other way now, don't mind me,* and immediately turn and head the opposite direction. Like I said, I'm not great with directions, and since I was just wandering, thinking I was the only person here, I can't remember exactly where the entrance is. As I'm retreating briskly, but still resisting the urge to run, I hear the man's voice and his footsteps coming up behind me. I'm trying not to think about how utterly alone I am here. About how I didn't see another person, car, or camel anywhere close to this fort. But I can't help it.

Fuck. That's all I can come up with to say to myself.

Meanwhile, the drunk man is so close behind me now I can smell his sour breath. Fearing I'm about to feel his hand on my shoulder, I turn and put up my own hand again. It is the same basic gesture, but this time it is a stop sign, not a hello. I haven't picked up enough Hindi to try to talk to him, and so all I can think to say is *No!* It is enough, though. He stops dead and then looks back at his companions, who are following at a distance. He repeats my command to them, *No!* Then they all start bending over laughing. I'm embarrassed, but use the pause to make my exit as quick as I can. Outside, I jump on the scooter, turn the key, and take off, without looking back to see if they are following. Of course, it's possible I have overreacted to their advances. But then again, what if I didn't. I decide that for the rest of the day I'll stick to exploring sights that are out in the open.

The island is not much of a tourist destination and is comprised almost entirely of locals. There are a few small villages to the west, a couple of public beaches to the south, a great deal of agricultural land and salt plains in the middle, and not much else. The guesthouses that are here are confined to the Eastern-most end of the island, in the tiny township of Diu, and they mostly cater to backpackers. Which is exactly why I decided to come here. There is clean air, open roads, and no tourist traps. Life is good.

Motoring up a small hill while coming back to the guesthouse from a visit to a mostly-deserted beach, just about half an hour before sunset, my scooter breaks down. *Okay smarty pants, what are you gonna do now? Mr. hot-shot third-world traveler. Well, I guess I'm going to start walking this broken scooter back in the direction of the guesthouse and hope I don't get eaten by a pack of wild dogs.* As I'm doing just that, two young men are heading the opposite way. They see me walking the bike and stop to investigate. They apparently speak no English, so we communicate by hand gestures and by smiles. One of them waits with me while the other goes to gather some tools. He returns, fixes the bike in less than 10 minutes, and though I thank him profusely, he refuses to take any money for the repair. Maybe this is the thing I've been looking for. Maybe it wasn't a person, an idea, or a thing, but a place.

Or maybe not. The next day is New Year's Eve. During the day, I wander the streets I haven't seen, go to the beach with some other backpackers, and take a short nap. At night, there is a party and there is music. There is dancing, there is a girl, and there is bhang chocolate. I have my own room. And we go there together. And still I blow it. Somehow, the two of us happy and naked in the dark on New Year's Eve. And I panic. And I back off. And we both spend what should have been a glorious night uncomfortably inhabiting the same room. And the next day I walk away. And I don't look back. Because I usually don't. And I'm an idiot. But I'm a free idiot. Without any strings. Without obligation. Without love. The barn door is wide open. And one thing I know how to do is run. All the way to India. And then some.

LE FEU DU CIEL

NUMBER SIXTEEN IN THE MAJOR ARCANA is *Le Feu du Ciel*, the Fire of Heaven. A phallic-shaped tower is being struck by a bolt of lightning and two figures, a male and a female, are falling from its heights.

Where the bolt strikes, gold coins fall to the earth. The image reveals our divine human nature. Spiritual consciousness often comes to us in an awakening flash.

–THE BOOK OF MYSTERIES

SCYLLA

He has used every resource the Dorje has gifted him along this path. Yet there are times when he must return to the small fire in his own heart to illuminate his way. Even now, exhausted, hungry, cold, and bruised, it does not fail him. Where the rain soaked kindle meets the swollen earth, against all probabilities he finds rock, leaf, and limb, sheltered and dry—protected treasures in an unprotected world—as if they were awaiting his arrival. He coaxes the spark, nurtures the flame, and then surrenders to sleep, his master's words swimming through his dreams.

Fire is the voice of god, speaking in tongues. Fire is the liberator of water, slipping the earthly bonds. Fire is the memory of stone, being released to the heavens. Fire is the mother of the Earth, born of desire. Fire is the seducer of wind, dancing in abandon for its beloved. Fire is the illuminator, the protector, the destroyer, and the giver of all life.

The Dorje understands that to find the heart of fire, we must go underground, into the world of passion, emotion, uncertainty, where we are most raw, unformed, authentic. To reach him in this state, the Dorje must journey to his dream world, and then lead him into her own, trailing with her an Ariadne thread. In the dream world, he must take the thread and use it to stitch together the inner and outer realms and to unravel a secret language long trapped between these worlds. Following her into her hidden world, new words flow from his lips, with the ease of water falling from cliffs. A new dimension opens, a new path through which all sentient beings may pass.

He does not know where the words will lead. Nor can he direct their course. He does not own the words any more than the river belongs to the rock, the earth, or even the Dorje. The sky did not create the water and does not know its course. He is the cloud and the stone. He is the lover and the beloved.

This is no small thing. This is the end and the beginning. The turning over. The new world being born.

PRAEDA

THE SHARP, cleansing smell of fire fills your awareness. Mixed with the offerings of incense and oils. Along with the rich smells of chapatti being cooked, chai being steamed, cow dung being burned for fuel.

You open your eyes and the old man with the silver coins has returned, bringing you fresh coals from another fire to light your hooka. You prime the pipe as the old man waits patiently. He wants to know more of the lions and their adventures. You decide to take him with you on the journey this time. When the smoke is ready, you offer him a seat on the cushion.

*　　*　　*　　*

A young prince sits on the bank of the Nerunjara River beneath the shadow of a crescent moon. He eats a small meal and leans back beneath a flowering tree. He is troubled by human suffering, and by the inevitability of sickness and death. So much so he has walked away from his future throne and his wealth. Everyday he comes to this place and he sits. Gradually the great fire fades into the earth and the silver of the moon steadily grows brighter. He looks for answers in both of them, and also all around him, in the flowers, the trees, and the stars in the sky.

One evening, after many days, he notices two lions on the opposite bank of the great river. The lions also lay beneath a small tree. He cannot tell from the distance whether they are watching him, but they face his direction. He imagines he and the lions are kindred. That, like him, they are searching the landscape for answers. This thought gives him comfort. Perhaps all beings struggle with this existence in their own way. His heart settles for the moment, and he gathers himself up and finds a place to sleep.

Each afternoon he returns to the tree beside the river, and as the sun begins to set, the lions join him. Each day he studies the Vedic verses and considers their counsel that he should escape the physical world. He follows these teachings, but finds no lasting comfort. He denies himself physical pleasure, but finds no peace. These exercises only bring him more discomfort.

The three companions continue their nightly ritual throughout the opening and the closing of the moon's eye. Then one day, as the young man sits beneath the Bodhi tree admiring one of its blood-red flowers, the separation between himself and the flower dissolves.

He sees that life does not lie behind a looking glass. The flower is still a flower, yet it is no longer only a flower. He sees that there is no need to seek to possess the beauty of the flower, to long somehow to be made whole by its beauty. Tree, river, flower, bird, lion, sky, moon, heart, raven, song, wave, leaf of grass, he ceases to see these things as individual items, separate from himself. And as he does, he sees them clearly for the first time.

Eventually, he looks across the river. The lions stand at attention. In their knowing gaze, he understands that beauty is inherent in all life. He sees that beauty's gift has always been there. He recognizes that happiness is found, not just in acceptance of the impermanence of everything, but in rejoicing in this fact. By reveling in the reality that beauty will never stop its intoxicating dance. And that freedom is the ability to love this second and the next equally.

The young man bows to his twin companions. They lower their heads in return. The would-be king eventually becomes known by many names, including Enlightened One, Buddha, and the Ninth Avatar of Vishnu. Though he writes down nothing, his stories and teachings are passed on by others. And though he cares nothing of this, there is poetic irony in that, had he remained a prince, with all his wealth and power, his story may never have been told.

CHARYBDIS

I wake up in Junagadh, back on the mainland. It is 5 am and the guesthouse proprietor's son is knocking on my door. I dress hurriedly and run downstairs. Remarkably, in the emptiness of the world before dawn, a single rickshaw sits across the street. I step in and tell him I want to climb the holy mountain. As we pull away from the curb and make our way through the silent streets, we are the only sign of life in the city.

*   *   *   *

I walk slowly up a seemingly endless set of stone steps. On the way up the path, set into the earthen walls of the mountain, there are shrines to one deity and then another. Brahma, Vishnu, Krishna, Shiva. They each sit in their own spaces carved into the wall. Small candles burn slowly, gracefully at the feet of each. As I have become accustomed to on this strange journey, I stop occasionally to pay homage. To light a candle. To give a small offering, a flower, a coin, tobacco, or a drop of water.

Next to one of the Shiva shrines, there is a tiny chai stall. Only a small dung fire illuminates the brass cooking vessel, the ladle, the face of the chai wallah. It is chilly out here in the darkness. And the cup is warm in my hands. So I sit for a few minutes, my hands overlapping each other around the tiny cup. When I am finished, I want to stay a while longer, to order another cup, and to just remain invisible in this darkness. But I don't. Instead, I stand up and bow a silent *Namaste* to the chai wallah. Before I turn uphill to continue the climb, the wallah spills something on his cooking fire, causing it to flare up. The flash of light illuminates the shrine and I see that at Shiva's left foot there is a lion. I have a feeling of *déjà vu* and pause for a moment to search my memory, to consider whether I'm dreaming again. Because the experience of India is so surreal anyway, it is difficult to know which it is.

I continue the slow, meditative journey up the mountain. There are a few others ahead of me and behind me, but not enough to erase the feeling of solitude. We all walk in silence and there is a deep feeling of reverence to the journey. It is still dark and I am clothed in linen and wrapped in an Indian shawl. So there are no visible signs that I am a Westerner, and no one gives any sign they have noticed.

The climb goes on for some time. It is a 10,000-step pilgrimage, after all. And I realize that the climb is like a car trip, in which you fall into a kind of meditative state and are not really aware of the passing of time. Until, that is, you finally arrive at your destination, and the car comes to a stop, pulling you out of your waking slumber, and suddenly you are aware not only of how far you've gone, and how long you've been in a trance, but that you weren't really ready to be wherever it is you are going.

At the summit, the sky is pink and orange and the sun is stretching its arms, preparing to pull back the covers and peek its head out over the horizon. In order to hang on to the quiet solitude for a while longer, I sit down on top of a large boulder, face the rising sun, and close my eyes. As the sun crests, I sit still beneath the shawl and let my body absorb the heat. I surrender to my senses and, for a time, I melt into the horizon. Becoming one with the sun's warmth, I drift and forget where I am.

After what may or may not have been a long while, my body warm, I get up, drop the shawl loosely around my shoulders, and begin my descent. As I make my way down the mountain, Indian pilgrims are still making their way to the top. The sun is now out, my shawl no longer covers my head, and I am looking people in the eyes, instead of following or being followed in the dark. And the attention I get from the loss of anonymity means it takes way longer to descend the mountain than it did to climb it. The looks of surprise from my fellow pilgrims tell me I may be the only Westerner on the mountain. Between the eager handshakes, the photos (with my camera), and the friendly invitations for tea, I begin to understand what a movie star in America might feel like when venturing into public. The mountain affords perspective.

LA TEMPERANCE

NUMBER FOURTEEN IN THE MAJOR ARCANA is called *La Temperance*. A sun-kissed winged woman holds two vases, pouring the contents of the upper into the lower, then continually reversing the action. The upper container is gold and the lower is silver. Not a drop is spilled in this endless transference.

So the life force of a human being flows between the polarities of positive and negative, the visible and the invisible, lifetime to lifetime. So the divine descends to the earthly realms and then ascends again. So the idea of scarcity is a farce. So the indulgence in excess is pointless.

–THE BOOK OF MYSTERIES

SCYLLA

Like a dream, a drink of water is misunderstood, ignored, taken for granted. The simplest things are overlooked. And yet, it is the simplest things that are the most essential.

Water is spirit incarnate. Without it, we cease to exist. Water shapeshifts. Water runs and flows. Water collects and finds stillness. Water freezes in its tracks. In ways unfathomable to our bodies of clay, water quietly breathes itself free of this visible plane.

We are uninspired by the simplicity of water and yet we are in awe of its power. We cannot comprehend the vastness of the ocean. We fear the unchecked rage of a river in flood. And there is no knowing when or where the next cloud will appear, the next thunderbolt will be cast, the next drop will fall.

The rain is a near constant companion on his journey. At any moment, he knows, a downpour can come, and a flood can wash away all life as he knows it. The river he calls his beloved could swell and threaten his very life. The rain casually continues its steady pace, drenching all he owns, and not letting up for day after day. The ground becomes like a clouded river.

Just when he is at the threshold of the Dorje's heart, he discovers he cannot make fire, cannot eat or keep warm. And yet, he also knows, without the rain he will not succeed. He needs the water to feed the river, to wash away his footprints, to give him reprieve from the punishing heat.

Water is patient. Water is not driven by fear, or ego, or attachment. Water has only one desire. To be water. And the importance of that is beyond words.

In order to cross the bridge, he must become like water. He must be both visible and invisible. He must flow from one form to the other. He must become a tantric master. He must embrace the river and become one with her. He must learn her secrets. And he must share with her his own. Without holding anything back for another day. There is no other day. There is only right now.

PRAEDA

You are swimming in the sea. Out on the horizon are several wooden fishing boats, with long oars extending into the water. Between you and the boats, you see three dark-colored porpoises, slowly arcing above and below the water. The sea is calm, and as they glide in and out, above and below, they cause ripples, which go on forever. The boats sit in the unusual stillness, rocking almost imperceptibly.

Soon, though, the rocking grows more noticeable and then more dramatic. Waves rise up from their slumber and march into battle, crashing down on your head and torso, tossing you about as you flail towards shore, which suddenly seems impossibly far away. You have a thought to catch hold of one of the dolphins, so that maybe it could pull you to safety, but they have all disappeared.

The pounding waves continue as the sky darkens and the boats become barely visible. Over and over you are swallowed by ocean and thrust back into sky. You try to keep straight when to hold your breath and when to gasp for air, but the separation between the worlds of above and below has become murky. Still you keep on, determined that you can somehow overcome these ridiculous odds. You lose track of which direction the finite safety of shore awaits and the infinite blackness of ocean stretches out into death.

Suddenly the ocean swells beneath you, and instead of being overwhelmed by its force, you are carried towards the shore on its crest. You are far above the surface of the water, like in a flying dream, held fast between the feelings of weightless freedom and abject terror.

This sensation continues as the crest continues to rise and fall, carrying you with it. But just as quickly as it lifted you up, it drops you. And you are free falling towards the blackness of the sky. Or the water. Or the shore. You have no way of knowing which.

And then something catches you and sets you down, without any impact at all, as if you were a baby being laid down to rest. You awake on the shore, lying on the sand in breathless bewilderment. A naked woman cradles your trembling form. Her crimson hair drips down your shoulders and your back. The waves gently lick your toes. The clouds shelter you from the sun's curious eyes. You can rest here. You are safe.

CHARYBDIS

I MAY HAVE MENTIONED I have this thing with lions lately, in my dreams. I'm not really sure why, but more than usual, these dreams blur the line between the worlds. I wake as a lion, I feel at home. I wake as a human, I am confused. I'm sure this has something to do with wanting to come here, to the Sasan Gir Lion Preserve, where as of this morning, betraying its namesake, I have yet to see any lions. Despite the obvious connection, I didn't intentionally come here to sort out this dream thing. I was compelled to come here, all the same, for reasons I don't fully understand.

The only official place to stay around here is at the hotel in the Preserve, which is priced like a resort, though it's really more like a dressed-up base camp for the wildlife preserve. There are Indian prices and Westerner prices for rooms. Unlike many places where this is true, but unspoken, the separate prices are actually written on a sign in the lobby. Which explains why I'm crashing in a local family's spare room, for a fraction of the cost. Turns out these are by far the most popular places to stay here for backpackers. But it isn't as if they're listed in guidebooks or have a webpage. So the only way to find these rooms is to ask around in the food stalls or to check with local chai wallahs.

While I am devouring a thali after another long and comfortless bus ride to get here, a backpacker from New Zealand plops down across from me at the table. After he orders and we go through the usual introductions, he asks if I have a place to stay. When I say not yet, and complain about the prospect of succumbing to the Westerner rate at the Preserve hotel, he invites me to share the room he is renting. That's how he found out about it a few days ago and he wants to pay it forward. Also, there might be a girl staying there for a night or two, he says, but there is a big bed and plenty of floor space, if needed.

The Kiwi has been to the Preserve twice and has seen several deer and even a six-point buck, but no lions. He says he's heard that there are locals, though, lion whisperers if you will, who know the lions' patterns and can almost guarantee a sighting. For a fee, of course.

Jaded as I am now by the tourist scams on the subcontinent, I decide I still prefer this approach to paying for an overpriced jeep ride to get the same results. So we ask around at the food stalls until we find our guide, a short and sinewy man who looks to be no older than his late twenties. He asks a reasonable fee, and earns credibility when he insists we meet no later than 5 am, as this is when the nocturnal beasts will be on their way home. This in contrast to the various jeep tours, all of which are during daylight hours.

Our request to be woken at such an unreasonable hour is met with some resistance by the owners of the room for rent, but when we explain why, they agree. For a fee, of course.

So here I am, up again in the pre-dawn Indian hours, creeping around in the forest. We're on foot, without any vehicle for protection, and also without so much as a flashlight. I have a headlamp, but our guide makes me turn it off. Which sends him down a peg or two on the credibility scale. I mean, we're trying to find something that will, without any doubt, see and smell us long before we see it. And this raises a question I wish I hadn't asked myself: *If I actually see a lion, will it be the last thing I see?*

The guide assures me that though we should treat the lions with due respect, the locals and the lions are able to peacefully coexist, even out in the middle of the Preserve. So we keep looking. Until sometime after the sun has come up. And still no lions have made an appearance. I'm not sure whether I am disappointed or relieved. We make our way back out of the Preserve and to the little town. Where we promptly sit down for a beer, even though it is probably before 9 in the morning. The Kiwi is leaving around noon to go down to Kerala. So we stay in the café, ordering more chapatti and more beers until it's time for him to pack and catch the train.

I stay in Sasan Gir. After three days and two more trips into the Preserve, I move on. But on the last morning in town, I go out with a different guide, on a new moon, near a known watering hole. When we arrive at the clearing for the water, I see a shadow dart from the pond and a thick tawny tail follow. I resolve to call this a sighting, or at least as close as I'm going get to one, and hop a train that day for a 25-hour ride all the way to South Goa— which everyone knows is not really India—completely bypassing Mumbai and all its big-city trappings. I grab a top bunk in a second-class car, wrap my arm through my backpack strap, and sleep, almost the whole way. Occasionally I wake up to the sound of a food cart, eat a masala dosa with my hands, then go back to sleep.

L'HERMITE

NUMBER NINE IN THE MAJOR ARCANA is called *L'Hermite*, the Hermit. An old monk is draped in a hooded cloak and holds a long wooden staff in his left hand. The staff is accented by seven burls along its length. In his right hand he carries a lamp, which is partially sheltered behind his cape.

The Ancient Mysteries must be protected from the storms of fear and ignorance. Just as the light of the spirit is concealed by human flesh. Yet, this light leaks out into the world through the cracks of words and deeds. Blessed be the keepers of the flame.

–THE BOOK OF MYSTERIES

SCYLLA

HE AWAKES WITH A STONE IN HIS HAND. He has no memory of how it came to be there. Or how long he has been asleep. Or even if he has been asleep. The stone is black, a deep, pure black. Its blackness would be absolute, except for a white spot on one side. Holding the stone, he can feel a pulse. Its vibration ripples through his hand, his arm, his chest.

When he stares into the spot, it is as if he is looking through a tiny keyhole, a secret doorway, into the eye of the universe. And he can feel it staring back at him, as if it is just as curious about him as he is about it. When he peers into this vastness of space, it is like he has peeled back a corner of his own skin and is staring into the vastness of his being. As if, just beneath his skin, is also an infinite universe.

The stone reveals to him what he has read many times, but has only partly understood, despite his repeated humble approaches. The stone shows him that his flesh, without which he could not navigate this physical world, is also a veil to what is real. *Our bodies are one more way in which the Universe organizes itself. They are windows for consciousness to see through.*

All at once he understands how the stone came to be in his possession. It is a second gift from Master Rinpoche.

PRAEDA

You ARE WALKING AFTER HER. Down through the narrow streets of little Babylon, past the cling, cling of bells and the waft of incense, through the maze of dust and the musk of camels. Up to the top of the horizon, where she threatens to drop out of sight. Until, without prelude, she stops and turns back towards you. She beckons. Silently. Patiently seducing you without words or gestures.

She knows the effect she has on you. She must. Knows you have no choice but to follow her. No matter her destination. You are mesmerized beyond explanation.

You lift your eyes again to the horizon. Though the sun threatens you with every upward glance. Then, at the top of the hill, you catch the first glimpse of them. Just above the bend of her knees, beside the curve of her long robes. At first, only a silhouette, a tuft of mane. One and then the other. As you climb higher, all four ears and both massive heads rise above the dust.

Though you have no idea their connection to each other, or what it has to do with you, you know this is no illusion, no dream. Their worlds have always been blended. Your worlds.

CHARYBDIS

I AM SITTING IN A CAFE SIPPING CHAI and staring at the Arabian Sea. I wear a lungi and not much else. I am barefoot, my toes rest in sand. It took more than a full day on a train to get here. I walked over two miles from the bus stop with my full pack in the midday sun. I tramped up and down the beach talking to different guesthouse owners. Many places were full. Some were too expensive. Others were simply unfriendly. But this one is perfect; little bungalows around a small courtyard lined with flowers, and weathered benches on each porch.

The rooms are rustic and basic, like most backpacker digs. Though there is a shower and bathroom included. And the property also has a little café off the front, at the edge of the beach. The woman who owns the place is also the cook. She makes me an omelet every morning, a masala omelet with the freshest eggs you've ever tasted. There are no ATMs here and I am out of cash. I gave the owner a deposit when I checked in and though she does not know me from any other scruffy, unwashed backpacker, she is letting me carry the balance on a tab until I can get to a bank for a credit card advance or some other form of financial miracle.

Three nights ago I met a young American who carries a backpack guitar, rolls a perfectly conical joint, and seems wise beyond his 18 years. I wake him up this morning on my way to breakfast. We skip my usual routine at the guesthouse and walk (barefoot) down the beach to a place with card tables spread out in the sand. We order some eggs and coffee, smoke a little hash, and watch the dolphins swim by in front of us. The rest of India and its hardships are far, far away.

* * * *

The kid and I rent scooters and go to a secret cove a few miles South of Goa. We spend the afternoon body surfing in the ocean waves and climbing around on the rocks on one end of the beach. Though we have no real plan, and brought only two bottles of water and two beers, we decide to spend the night here. We catch crabs with our bare hands and cook them over a campfire left hot by local fishermen. We drain the beers, and when the fire burns out, we go to sleep on the beach, covered up with our lungis.

The next day, we walk up to the only café in the tiny fishing village. For about 50 cents, we dine like kings on the fishermen's morning catch, with rice, a bowl of masala sauce, and a cold beer. Again, I think, *Maybe this is the thing, this place.*

* * * *

The American is not the only companion I've collected since I've been on this beach. The morning after I arrived, I was sitting in my Indian mom's cafe, sipping chai and staring at the Arabian Sea, wearing a lungi and not much else, sand beneath my toes, when a young Indian woman—almost too old to still be selling fruit on the beach—approaches me and asks if I want a henna tattoo. That isn't all she says, but that is the point. She is clever and so she makes conversation, pretends to be interested in why I am here and where I come from.

Like most young Indian women, she is striking. She also moves and speaks with a healthy measure of self-confidence. She knows her game, knows she does not have the benefit of childlike cuteness, like the children all around her who sell trinkets on the beach. And she knows she cannot come off as too grown-up either, or she'll be taken for a prostitute, which she definitely is not. She is somewhere between these two worlds. And she plays her self-invented role in this in-between world with ease and grace.

Though I started out in India naïve and a bit doe-eyed, this many weeks into my journey I've developed my share of wariness against being scammed. But I also possess something many backpackers don't, a willingness to pay a little something extra for an intentional experience, to follow an interesting stranger, to take a road less sure, just to see where it might lead. And so, with open eyes, the girl and I have become friends, in our own way.

I paid her for a henna tattoo during that first meeting, of course. But I've also secured her daily companionship by promising to buy 200 rupees worth of fruit from her everyday while I am here. This is an experience worth every bit of the less than five dollars a day I pay for it. Because it means that several times a day, all the trinket-selling children on the beach sit down in a circle with us, and I ask different ones to choose which fruit to cut open. Then she cuts the pineapple or the watermelon or the mangoes and we pass the slices around to all the little hands and mouths. While we eat, I ask them to tell me about their day so far. For a few moments, I am not a Westerner for them to sell things to, and they can forget their hustle and just be children eating fruit on the beach. It is a wonderful and unique communion that I could not have expected or maybe even imagined.

Eventually, the girl's family invites me to dinner. I walk the half-mile down the beach to their hut. It has an A-framed roof and is no taller than six feet at its center. It sits on the side of a dry ravine, a hundred yards or so from a touristy beachside restaurant. I am invited inside, to sit on the dirt floor and eat. There is a tiny fire pit at one end, where all meals are prepared. Pots and bags of clothes and other sundry are hung around the tops of the walls. The food is good, simple, spicy, and fresh. They offer me bottled water, but I drink from their pitcher instead.

I have no illusions about why I am here. Because I am an American, they believe I have more money than I do. I have been unsuccessful so far at convincing any Indians, including them, that I am not wealthy. I know I'm here because they would like to charm me into giving them some kind of a gift, gold jewelry for the girl's dowry or something of like value. But they are also genuinely nice to me, all the same. They are curious about who I am, where I come from, and what I do for a living. And as I've explained, I am willing to pay something for the experience, even if it turns out I am not the captain of the ship they imagine me to be.

Her father and her sister's husband are outside chewing paan, where the children are playing. Her sister continues cooking over the fire. Only the girl sits briefly to eat a little food with me. I eat with my hands, as I have been doing virtually since I landed on the subcontinent. Occasionally, the girl corrects my technique. It is a strange mixture of tenderness and scrutiny.

I feel at once honored by the invitation to this humble feast and also somehow unworthy. Though I have been honest about my means, I know they do not believe me. Ultimately, I know I will not meet their expectations. Should I then refuse their invitation? Forgo this experience? The answers are not easy to come by. Perhaps I take solace in the fact that I am already doing what I can to support them.

*   *   *   *

The family invites me to go inland with them. Apparently they have a small farm in Karnataka. In all, I've gone almost three weeks without shoes, and I'm not that thrilled about putting them back on. But I came here to find something. And I don't know where it will be. So until a voice inside warns me otherwise, I am willing to follow the threads that are laid out for me.

The morning of our departure, as I walk down the beach to their hut at dawn, there is a full moon hanging above the ocean horizon to the west and a sun just coming up in the east. Two perfect spheres watching over me. A perfect balance of the universal masculine and feminine.

*   *   *   *

It is a long, hot ride inland, on another bus with no shocks. We stop a few times at roadside cafés, to take restroom breaks and for snacks. At each stop, wallahs selling peanuts and pakoras in newspaper cones hawk their edibles through the open bus windows. The family's youngest son tugs at me to buy him something at every stop. On the third leg of the journey, the heat, the fried food, and the constant jars and jolts prove too much for the boy, and he throws up on me. His father hands me a cloth to clean it off my arm, but no one seems too surprised or concerned by this small indignity.

I stay at their house in Karnataka for three days. I sleep on the floor, on a pallet of sorts, in a big main room with the rest of the family. During the days, I am walked around the town and introduced to family after family. I discover that I am only the second white person most people in the town have met, both of us delivered by my host family. To refuse what is offered at these visits would be an unthinkable insult, and so I am stuffed so full of puffed rice and other snacks by the end of each tour that I can hardly move.

I go to the fish market and to the produce markets and, since I cannot speak their language, the only thing for me to do is to watch them carefully in their dealings with each other. No exchange is straightforward. Everything is a conversation, a negotiation, a process of bargaining. And, whether it is to prove a point for future bargaining, or some other reason unknown to me, sometimes they walk away without completing the deal. No one seems terribly upset by this.

The second day, they walk me over to a nearby plot, where a concrete foundation has already been poured. They explain as well as they can that this house will be for the girl and her future family. Then, almost directly afterwards, they take me to visit someone who appears to be a banker. And the picture becomes more clear.

The banker speaks perfect English and fills me in on their exact expectations, even giving me an account number where I can wire money for the project. So now I am in the middle of nowhere India, without any idea how to get to the next town, and at the mercy of a family who have expectations I can't possibly meet.

Though I really have no idea what to say, I try again to explain. I am traveling in India because I'm not a rich American. And India is quite affordable compared to Europe. But people everywhere hear what they want to hear and believe the same.

Probably as a result of the stress of this new development, I have a terrible allergic reaction to something. For the rest of the day, I am reduced to sneezing and blowing my nose on the stash of toilet paper I retrieve from my backpack. There are no allergy tablets or other store-bought Western remedies here. Instead, the family matriarch prepares a special concoction for me, but it isn't for me to eat or drink. She stands me in her kitchen and passes a pan containing the red, steaming hot liquid up and down the length of my body. She does this three times, while chanting something I don't understand. I lie down on the floor immediately after dinner and sleep like I'm dead until after the sun comes up.

The next morning I convince the family I must leave to meet a friend in a town called Hampi. Alone on the bus and extricated from this latest entanglement, I feel better almost immediately. Once again, I am free. I don't think that was the thing.

LE DIABLE

NUMBER FIFTEEN IN THE MAJOR ARCANA is called *Le Diable*, the Devil. A winged creature that is half man, half ram holds an inverted scepter with a lighted torch at one end. The figure stands upon a gray sphere. Two beautiful naked satyrs, a male and a female, stand elegantly bound to the sphere by a golden chain that is loose about their necks.

The shadows of the satyrs are cast behind them and dissolve into the image of the creature. The flame of the scepter illuminates a doorway in the background. Though it is easier than we think to lose our way, all light is reflective.

–THE BOOK OF MYSTERIES

SCYLLA

THE SUN HAS BUT HALF A MEANING *without the shadow it casts into the ocean of the world. Likewise, a man is more than his thoughts. More than his actions or words. He is more than his highest intentions, his best and worst days. Each prayer we conjure says something about who we are.*

To say he is a monk, as simple as that, is incorrect. To say he is without desire is no less untrue.

Each cloud we burst, each moon we drum, each sun we dance is an essential part of the wheel. Though they are not the whole circle of our being. The whole is incalculable.

Beauty loves contradiction. Beauty is born of desire. And without beauty, there is nothing. Beauty is our keeper, our master, our reason. Beauty is illumination born of the dark.

The moon casts a different face everyday. Yet the moon is always the moon. It is always whole. Always reflective. A monk lives in simple robes, wraps himself in silence, eats food he pulls from the soil, reads from ancient codices. Yet a monk is always more than this. Without understanding the murderer inside the monk, enlightenment is not possible. Without the knowledge of desire, the purity of oneness remains out of reach.

It is not possible for the solely pious to enter into the hidden lands.

One must pass through the womb in order to live. The bright side of the moon could not exist without the half wrapped in shadow. A half-life is not substantial, not sustainable. You cannot cut out half your heart and live.

*　　*　　*　　*

The Dakini visits him at night. She removes his tattered robes with her deft fingers and bathes him in her sacred oils. Her soft kisses tickle his skin from his crown to his toes. She is a tantric master. She gives him refuge in her delicate art. She opens a portal in his heart of hearts. Without her, he could not find the illuminated heart he has been seeking all these months, these years, this life.

PRAEDA

You are in a grand cathedral. Light is diffused overhead through colored windows. On either side, there are more windows reaching from celling to floor. Despite this, the light is dimmed, as if it were filtered through clouds. As if it were caught between the worlds of night and day.

A large figure in a dark crimson robe stands on a dais before you, a book splayed in one hand, the other pointing to the sky. Incense burns in silver chalices set on pedestals on either side of the robed figure. Another figure in a white robe carries a glass half-filled with a deep red liquid towards the dais, then bows on one knee, holding up the glass. Words are spoken, a hand waved over the glass, and the figure in white stands again and walks in your direction.

There are black and white birds perched in the rafters and on pedestals of various heights throughout the cathedral. There are several larger gray birds flying overhead, and they cause the already-strained light from the windows above to bend and hide beneath their flying shadows.

You hear no sound at all. Though you feel a great vibration in the room. As if a mighty chorus were singing to the sky, but your ears could no longer hear the music. You cannot see behind you, but you sense there is a room full of people there, dancing, singing, and praying.

A parade of others, cloaked in red robes, appears from behind you, walking single file up the aisle, scattering flower petals along their path, the dais, and at your feet. The figure in white appears in front of you and bends to offer you the glass of wine. You raise your head and start to lift a hand to accept it, when you realize your hands are bound together with shackles of gold.

Just then, a figure in a black robe appears on your left. The figure gestures to the one in white, lifts you to your feet, and swiftly ushers you around behind her side of the dais. The dark figure places a hand on the shackles at your wrists and they immediately dissolve away. Then she pulls back the hood from her face just enough for you to see the green of her eyes, as she opens a hidden door and leads you through it.

CHARYBDIS

I AM IN A TOWN CALLED HAMPI, floating across the Tungabhadra River in something that looks and feels like a giant upside down acorn cap. I feel like Winnie the Pooh when he and Christopher Robin are floating through the flood waters in an upside down umbrella. The guides who captain these tiny vessels get 10 rupees a head to cross the river, so they tend to squeeze as many people as possible into each trip.

Hampi is a holy city in the state of Karnataka. A very long time ago, this was the capital of the Vijayanagara Empire. These days, it is not the capital of anything. In fact, there are only two buses a week traveling through here: Tuesdays and Fridays.

Being a holy city means that there are ancient Hindu temples here which are protected by international heritage organizations. It also means that bhang is sold here.

Bhang is a hash preparation which is used in religious ceremonies in India. Despite its sometimes use as an intoxicant, bhang is actually classified as an Ayurvedic medicine and not a drug. Whatever they call it, whether rolled into balls, dipped in chocolate, or mixed into a yoghurt lassi, it gives a pretty good buzz. Bhang is considered by some Hindus to be a gift from Lord Krishna, though it is often used in the worship of Shiva. How's that for gratitude? But back to the river, and this oversized acorn cap which threatens to slip beneath the water with me in it.

*　　*　　*　　*

185

This place is very relaxed. And very isolated. No trains travel here, so the only way in or out is a very long bus ride. This keeps the tourist traffic and the baksheesh beggars to a minimum. After a week of hard travel and the stickiness of the Goa family, I can finally relax again.

For the first time in at least four weeks, there are no demands on my time or my money. For the first time since Jaisalmer, I am without traveling companions. In other words, I am free again. I wake at dawn and go for runs through the town, along the river and out towards the ancient ruins, coming back as the shop keepers are starting to sweep away yesterday's energies from their store fronts and write today's blessings in chalk on the dirt ground. I rent a bicycle and ride through the ancient ruins. I wear a lungi and not much else. I go barefoot again, as much as possible. I read books and hang out in cafes. I take naps. I watch the Indian women in their colorful saris hand wash clothes by the river. I drink an occasional bhang lassi. I am not concerned with what comes next.

And then she appears. With long dark hair, green eyes, a European accent, and an untraceable heritage. Wearing gauze skirts and simple tank tops, sipping chai, and reading Kathryn Harrison. She has an almost preternatural ability to show up wherever I am, the chai wallah, the food stall, the upstairs cafe. Despite the intrigue I feel, I refuse to engage her. I have finally managed to untangle myself, to exist here without strings. And I want to keep it that way.

But she finds the gate to my secret garden anyway. She waits until the sun is down and I'm upstairs finishing a korma and sipping a bhang concoction. She comes out of a corner, like some kind of phantom, and slips quietly onto the bench across from me.

She doesn't speak at first. Instead, she reaches over without asking and takes a sip of my lassi, her lips lingering on the tip of the straw just a moment longer than necessary. Then she looks up at me and says, *And then what happened?*

Just like that.

In my favor is the surprising clarity which the bhang provides. Weighing against me is her intoxicating presence. I do my best to lean on the former. To turn down the voice of my second chakra. *She realized she had mistaken him for someone else, someone who was looking for a dinner companion.* I answer, with uncharacteristic calm and wit.

Who are you hiding from? Comes her second attempt.

Who says I'm hiding?

Well, aren't you?

If I am hiding, it's from no one in particular.

Not even yourself?

Who are you?

Who do you want me to be?

Where did you come from?

You should know; it was apparently you who summoned me here.

Summoned? Seriously, who are you? Who talks like that?

She doesn't answer. Instead, she takes another sip of my drink. And then she says, *Come on, let's go for a walk.*

I need to pay the check, I plead. As if going with her were suddenly a foregone conclusion, despite my resistance. *When did that happen?* I wonder.

It's settled already. She says in a calm, matter-of-fact voice.

We descend the stairs and walk together through the dimly lit streets and past the chai stalls and the closed shops. It's safe to say I have no idea what I am doing. It's as if she has dared me to come with her and I have accepted the dare, simply to show I'm not a coward.

We are walking mostly side by side, but she is definitely leading. We wander out of reach of the lights of the small village and down towards the river. We say almost nothing, which feels both natural and uncomfortable. When we reach the water, she leans back against a large boulder. The half moon is suspended over the water, making sparkle everything with any thought of reflectivity, turning the landscape of river and rocks into a field of diamonds shimmering in the darkness. She looks up at me from her resting place and her eyes mirror the moon's tricks.

What is it you want? She asks, simply, sincerely.

Shouldn't that be my line? I ask. *Didn't you seek me out?*

You've come here looking for something. But you won't find it if you don't know what it is. You won't find it if you can't name it.

You're very sure of yourself. How do you know what I've named? I answer.

Even if that's so, you won't find it if you don't know how to ask for it.

That completely disregards serendipity, you know.

Perhaps. Or it could be you hide behind vague, mystical notions like that to avoid taking full responsibility for your life.

You say something like that and yet you seem like someone who believes in magic, depends upon it even.

You don't seem like a guy who has trouble with words, so why can't you name your desire? With this, she unwraps the delicate scarf from around her neck and places it on the rock next to her. Next she steps out of her shoes, one foot at a time and caresses the sand with her toes.

Are you afraid if you admit what you want, you might have to risk not getting it? You might have to look failure in the face and admit that you borrowed his coat?

That's a little trite, isn't it?

Is it? If it is, it's only because there are only four or five human stories... She continues to play in the sand with her toes. Then she lifts her hair off her neck, twisting and resting it on one shoulder.

And what is yours?

What do you want it to be? She is at once mysteriously cagey and also completely transparent. I have no box to put her in.

Does it matter what I want?

Yes, it does. She says, as she stands again, taking a step in my direction. And then another, until she is right in front of me. She stares up into my face, examining it, searching my eyes for something. Not in a dreamy way, but not cold either, interested, curious. Then without hesitation she slides her right hand behind my head, reaches up, and kisses me. Her kiss is warm, wet, open. Passionate, but not overly eager. It is as if, in that brief moment when she was searching my eyes, she discovered exactly how I wanted to be kissed. And then she kissed me just like that. Like even I could not have known I needed to be kissed.

I meet her kiss and move her body slowly backwards, towards one of the large boulders where her scarf still lays. I lean our bodies gently back against the smooth rock and reach for her hands, her wrists, her arms, her waist.

We fall to our knees in the sand, hidden from the world by the giant rocks, the sounds of the river. She pulls my t-shirt up and tugs it over my head, kissing my bare shoulders, my neck, my mouth. Then she leans back and pulls her own shirt over her head, revealing her breasts in the moon's candlelight. Slowly, but eagerly, we begin the feast. We start to envelope each other, to take on each other's skin.

When we finally come to rest, I help her up and wrap her loosely in her discarded clothes. We move quickly back to my room, where we immediately drop our gathered clothes and start again. We continue on into the night, until sleep overcomes us both.

When I wake up, the sun has already been at work for hours. Bright beams press themselves under cracks and through worn curtains. I turn away from the window and towards the door. In my half-sleep the night before comes rushing back at me, and all at once I realize I am the only one in the bed. Though I am looking directly at the empty side of the bed where she lay before, I reach out my hand anyway, to touch the bare sheets.

For a moment I wonder if I have blurred dreams and reality again. Then the door creaks open and she sneaks back in, her wrap-around skirt pulled up over her chest. I watch her bare feet come towards me across the concrete floor. When she reaches the bedside, she sets down two small cups of chai. And then she drops her wrap and slips back under the sheets with me. I'm pretty sure I'm dreaming.

Ounce for ounce, inch for inch, grace for grace, she has to be the most beautiful creature I've ever seen. Surely I'm dreaming.

*   *   *   *

We stay in the room, making love and napping, until the sun has nearly set again. Hunger finally drives us out into the shadowy streets. We find a food stall that serves thalis and devour two plates and a half dozen chapati. We drink more chai and when we are finished, we go for another walk down to the river.

When we get to the place where the boulders are, where all this delicious indulgence began, where we are sheltered from the eyes of the town, she begins to undress again, dropping her clothes as she goes. She is standing by the river bank in the light of the half moon and I am paralyzed by her beauty. Then she turns to me and says, *Come on, let's take a bath.* And she walks into the water, holding out her hand to me.

Without much thought or hesitation, I, too, shed my skin and follow her into the river. If I thought she couldn't get any more beautiful, I was wrong. Glistening wet and sparkling in the moonlight, she is a goddess touched down on Earth. I don't have any idea what is going on anymore. I don't know if I'm dreaming. And I don't care. If none of this is real, I never need to know. I have reached Satori. I have touched the Sun. I have disappeared into the soul of the Universe.

*   *   *   *

It is Friday, mid-morning and we are having breakfast upstairs, in the same cafe where we officially met. After the omelets are gone, we order more chai. Then she realizes she forgot to bring her money and says she wants to treat. She asks for the key to the room and says she'll be right back, then we can finish our tea and plan our adventures for the day.

She never comes back.

After 10 minutes, I begin to worry if she is ok. But I think she is probably cleaning up, or has stopped along the way to get some little surprise. I wait for almost 20 minutes until finally I pay the bill and head back to the room. The door is locked when I get there. I knock but there is no answer. Eventually, I find the owner and explain that I think I left my key in the room. He looks mildly annoyed as he uses his passkey to open the door. He reminds me there is a fee for a replacement key.

I thank him and close the door behind me. The room looks much like it did when we left. I look around. I check the bathroom. I look in the closet. No sign of her. Then I pull my backpack out of the corner and notice that the contents are upset, like they have been pulled out and stuffed back in, hurriedly. Which leads me to my next thought. I scramble under the bed and look to where I stashed my cash belt. My mind pushes back the size of the disappointment that looms unavoidably in its path. I look again, checking different corners, scanning my memory just as furiously to see if I may have moved it to another hiding spot. But I know I didn't.

And then I remember that it's Friday. I bolt for the door and run at full speed the several blocks to the bus station. Out of breath and crazy-eyed, I ask the man behind the counter when the next bus is scheduled to leave. Looking amused, he says, *Next Tuesday, eleven o'clock.* I search the wall for the schedule and check the clock. According to the log, the last bus left 15 minutes ago.

*   *   *   *

Adrenaline seeps from my veins all at once, draining into the invisible underworld. I scuff my way through the dirt streets for a while, stopping in a small chai stall. Not knowing what to do next. An old and wrinkled man in a dingy blue shirt serves me a scalding hot glass of chai as he tells me I am looking more forlorn than usual. I don't recognize him. I don't remember stopping here before. I still don't know if I am awake or dreaming.

That is because somewhere, in this life or another, I must have sinned greatly. And now I am being punished for it. I answer.

Ah, says the man. *Be not too hard on your former self then. Remember instead what the Buddha said: A pious man cannot find his way into the hidden lands.*

I look at him with eyes full of questions. I am no longer sure of anything.

LA FORCE

THE NUMBER ELEVEN IN THE MAJOR ARCANA is called *La Force*, Strength. A young woman dressed in white robes stands with her hands on the head of a lion. Her head is adorned with a wreath of white flowers, in which sacred birds and serpents rest. Over her floral crown floats the symbol of Infinite Love.

Passion must join forces with Compassion, so the inner flame can enhance the power of the sun. Grace holds space for Knowledge to be transformed into Courage, Lust to shine its light, and Surrender to ascend its throne. These are keys she holds to the door of Secret Wisdom.

–THE BOOK OF MYSTERIES

SCYLLA

He awakens. Troubled by his surrender to desire. By thoughts that he has failed to transcend. *As inside, so outside.* The land mirrors the impasse in his mind. The gorge before him is deeper than the human heart. The walls around him are taller than the sky. He looks back and cannot see the path that led him to this locked door.

A fog lays heavy. The moon is cloaked. The fire a pale memory. He contemplates whether he is at this journey's end. He sits silent. Closes his eyes. Finds the stillpoint. He accepts being lost. He lets go of the rope.

Time passes by like so many rapids in the river. Unable to tell when it begins, where it ends, how far it has gone. In the half-light of dawn, he finds the space to reflect upon the fullness of the night's dream. And then, in the stillness of that silence, he laughs.

He understands his dream companion is actually the goddess of the land herself, the Dorje, come to guide him along her hidden path. Come to reveal her doorway. Come to remove the veils with his robes. Come to reveal her secret heart.

As inside, so outside. He follows her along the hidden passage to her secret heart, which lies beneath the falls. To the place where the water lets go. His knees find their place. His head bends to drink. As water pours over him, he remembers. *There is weakness in resistance, strength in letting go*. His surrender has made them one again. The door is open.

For a time, he is euphoric. Slowly this fades. As water through fingers. He is emptied. Only lightness remains. And the infusion of space. Then a wave of calm. A gentle aftershock. It does not crash over him. But washes into him. Filling him up. Infusing his cells. He understands the sense in paradox.

The dreamer holds the dream and surrenders the words.

Enlightenment is not the absence of feeling. Not the ability to ignore sadness. It is a traverse of this opening and closing, these feelings of joy and emptiness. It is the path and the pinnacle. It is understanding there is weakness in resistance. Strength in letting go. Only the heart knows the way.

PRAEDA

THE SOUND OF RAIN FILLS YOUR EARS. Rain dancing on the hard ground. Rain drumming on the metal roof. Rain thundering down on the forests of grass. The smell of rain fills your nose, your head, your lungs. The memory of flowers, fresh pools of water, and wet birds, all rush in on your senses.

You open your eyes and watch the barrage of tiny explosions as the army of droplets surrender to the Earth's eternal pull, then write their names in concentric circles, forever colliding, merging with dirt and blade and each other.

From the shadows of the horizon, two figures rush forward, seeking refuge under your humble sail. It is the old man with the round face, this time with his grandson. The boy brushes water from his face, fishes a coin from his satchel, and holds it out for you. You bow, thank him, and begin.

*   *   *   *

Many years pass after the would-be king discovered a different way of seeing the Bodhi flower. In all this time, though, his message did not spread far from the tree. It was, like so many others, a tumultuous time. There were explorations and conquests, wars and killing, oppression and subjugation.

In time, a powerful dynasty arose in the great triangle of land known then as Indus. At the head of the dynasty was a king named Chandragupta. In the vacuum left by Alexander the Great's unexpected death in Babylon, Chandragupta flourished. He amassed more territory than any other empire in the history of the land. It is not his story that is remembered, however, but that of his grandson, Ashoka.

For a while, Ashoka did nothing remarkable. He simply followed in his father's and grandfather's footsteps. Ashoka was not the eldest of his brothers. One day, however, his father, Bindusara, sent Ashoka a message that the territory belonging to his elder brother, Susheema, was in trouble. An uprising had grown beyond his brother's control. When Ashoka arrived, he discovered that the unrest was a plot by several ministers in his brother's government to take over power.

Ashoka seized the ministers and made public examples of them. Then, to restore faith in his father's rule, he hosted an enormous feast for the citizens. There were dancers and music and plays and roasted lambs and wine and song continuing for several days and nights.

Consumed by accomplishing the task assigned to him, Ashoka failed to see the humiliation his brother would endure over his younger brother's handling of the crisis. Susheema knew the incident had cost him the family crown.

On the eve of Ashoka's coronation, while he was being prepared for the ceremonies, Susheema gathered a small army of assassins and marched towards the family castle under the cover of night. Ashoka, unaware of his brother's plans, but anticipating his arrival for the coronation, had prepared a special place for him. He had fountains and flowers and beautiful maidens ready to greet him, along with a pre-coronation feast.

Ashoka planned to name Susheema as his first minister and closest advisor, to give him a place in the castle and put him in charge of *a larger territory. But these plans would never come to fruition, as Susheema could not see through his own jealousy and hatred. Word of Susheema's plan spread ahead of him. Upon his approach, three scouts loyal to Ashoka infiltrated the elder brother's small army and killed Susheema along with two of his generals.*

Ashoka was devastated by his brother's death and by the revelation of his intentions. The coronation was delayed for two weeks while he mourned. After that, Ashoka put aside his heart in all matters of his empire and set his sights on the final piece of Indus, the kingdom of Kalinga.

Ashoka set out for Kalinga, but at night he began to have troubling visions of lions with unusual gifts and strength. He would awake not knowing whether he had dreamt them or not. In the darkness, he would hear their deep, thunderous calls. He could not separate the dreams from reality.

Soon the dreams became more intense. He prowled with the lions on their nocturnal journeys, accompanied them on their hunts, saw their ferocious power. He awoke sweating and trembling from one dream in which he became their prey. Then one night, out past the evening fire at his encampment, Ashoka caught the flash of huge eyes, the swish of a long tail. He rose to meet the sight, but found nothing there.

The next morning, after another night of restless sleep, he arose before dawn and found a trail of blood leading from his tent to a slaughtered lamb. He recognized the musky scent of a male lion.

The slaughtered lamb inside their camp caused a stir with his troops. So Ashoka sent out two of his best hunters with orders to return with the skins of any lions within a day's range. And he set his mind back upon Kalinga. But his hunters came back empty handed.

*　　*　　*　　*

The citizenry of Kalinga was armed and ready for Ashoka's arrival. They fought with courage and tenacity. And the battle lasted for many days. But they were finally outnumbered, and Ashoka's legions prevailed.

Ashoka rode through the fields of battle and into the streets of Kalinga to survey his new territories, the flag of victory raised high above his head. But his heart did not feel victorious. He had now achieved his ultimate dream. He expanded his territory to the farthest reaches he could imagine. But his victory seemed a hollow one.

He rode between the dead bodies strewn wherever he could see. He saw rivers of blood stain the soil and water of his land. For the first time in his adult life he knew shame. He knew his greed had caused unspeakable pain. How could the children who remained in this land ever look upon him as a great leader? How could he be their protector?

As the sun began to fall from the sky, Ashoka left his military escorts and rode towards the nearby foothills. He rode up to meet the setting sun and to ask the great warrior of the sky for an answer as to why so much blood had been shed for the sake of one man's vanity.

As he crested a peak beyond the sight of the others, he was met by two other kings. Two male lions, the size of which he had never seen, stood before him. Their massive chests pressed forward, their manes flowing in the invisible river of wind. But it was their eyes he would remember, eyes that shone with the light of a million candles.

*   *   *   *

Ashoka and his troops stayed on in Kalinga for months, rebuilding what they had destroyed, giving assistance to its citizens, and assigning some of his finest leaders to restructure the government and to build upon its prosperity.

Eventually, Ashoka returned to his home. He shut himself away for several months, fasting, studying Buddhist texts, and summoning its teachers. He put his advisors in charge of everything during this time. When he finally emerged, all spoke of his transformation. He was filled with light and beauty. He could bring a sense of calm to others simply by being in their presence.

His first commission was the building of a great pillar inscribed with the teachings of Buddha from top to bottom. And at the very top, were the carved figures of two mighty lions.

Over the next several years, similar pillars went up everywhere in the Mauryan Empire. Each inscribed with these same poetic tenets. In this way, the word of peace was spread. Ashoka's essential message to his people was carved in stone throughout the land: The only true victory is the one of the heart.

Ashoka changed his behavior in as many ways as he could. He vowed against violence of every kind. He even became a vegetarian. He set out on a series of missions to remote areas of the empire, not as a conqueror this time, but to develop numerous social programs to help those regions thrive. Everywhere he spoke to the people of his new designs and erected inscribed pillars as eternal messages of compassion and wisdom.

But Ashoka did not make the mistake of turning Buddhism into a national religion. Instead, he enacted a policy of widespread religious tolerance. And he did not become a monk, but remained the ruler and leader of his land and people. Perhaps the first and only philosopher king.

More than any other leader in history, Ashoka was able to integrate his spiritual beliefs into his daily life. The king and the land were one. And so the land and the people under Ashoka knew the greatest peace and prosperity they have ever known. Centuries later, many of his pillars still stand as symbols of the unity of the age.

CHARYBDIS

I HAVE A SECRET POCKET ON THE INSIDE of my backpack. The zipper hidden beneath a seam in one of the sides. The fabric is thick enough to conceal things like a passport and a reasonable amount of cash. The opposite side is padded, to assist in the illusion. My passport and credit card have been sealed in this pocket since I arrived in town and checked into my room. Along with a small amount of cash. But most of the cash I withdrew in Goa was still in the cash belt, except for what I had in my pockets at breakfast. It isn't enough for her to retire from being a grifter, but it is enough to send me back home early.

The money wasn't technically mine to begin with; it was borrowed. This habit I have of hiding started long before I came to India. Before that, I was in graduate school, which is as good a way as any to hide from the world. And, with an undergrad degree in philosophy, I had to do something. Because there's no place to post a diploma in a dishwasher's station, I figured graduate school would offer a more promising future. Also, it was an excuse to hide a while longer from the clock-punching, rush-hour-battling, quietly desperate world of career life. Having spent a good deal of my college money on aged port and used books, and grad school being twice as expensive as the bachelor variety, I had to borrow. And since I was going to have to get in bed with the moneychangers anyway, I decided I might as well borrow enough for a nice bed.

And then, well, I put grad school on hold for a while. Anyway, India is a better education than you can get in any school.

*   *   *   *

It's just past dawn, the day after the apocalypse of the heart, and I'm sitting in a café. Not the one where I met her. I don't think I can go back there, not even to wallow. Not even as a fuck-you. I want to though, because it's the only place in town to get a bhang lassi. And I need its special blend of numbing clarity right now.

If I hadn't screwed up on the island, panicked like I did, I might still be with the Welsh girl with the charming accent. And we'd be someplace else, floating on boats in Kerala, maybe. And then there wouldn't have been a window for the green-eyed goddess to climb through with her hammer. And my heart would never have been laid out on the table for her to smash into sea glass-sized pieces. And I'd have money for boat rentals.

I stayed outside most of the day yesterday, either in chai stalls or just walking the dusty streets, sitting by the river, watching the sun ease its way across the sky. Until it was dark and the lights of the cafés went out one by one. I must have passed out from exhaustion. But I woke up early and couldn't get back to sleep. And all the books in the world couldn't get me to stay in my room alone right now. So I find myself up, dressed and walking down the street even before the café opens, causing me to walk casually by the entrance, as if I weren't waiting to eat.

Once they are open and I'm inside, I order an omelet because, despite my lack of hunger, I read once that protein helps with depression. Even though I can't get enough of the masala dosa. And dosas I can eat with my hands. Like I've said, I eat as much as possible with my hands here. It's strangely liberating. I've watched older Indian men, dressed in western clothing, carefully balancing their neatly cut breakfasts on silverware, while across the room I sit, a white guy in ragged linen, eating a dosa with his hands.

The food arrives and I decide this is no time to start using silverware. But just as I pinch off a bite of my omelet with my fingers, an overwhelming sadness blows through a shattered window in my heart. I realize I am eating another meal alone. Surrounded by strangers. No one else to order with, to feed bites. No one to eat half the breakfast, so I won't be so full.

All at once, I become so unexplainably sad and tired that I literally lose the will to live. It just dissolves into my plate like melting butter into toast. And I no longer even want to lift my hand to my mouth. All I want is to lie down here, right here. On the chairs. Across the table. Maybe the floor, if I can get there. And die.

I even wonder if it's possible. To die right here. If anyone would mind or if they'd make me move somewhere less conspicuous. Even in remote India, a dead person in your restaurant is probably not good for business. I'm sure there are places in this country where it would be possible, but probably not here.

I feel my throat tighten and my eyes begin to swell. Another me takes over. This me lifts the small coffee cup from the table to my mouth and instinctively I drink. Then I turn my head to the book on the table. There are words underlined. I'm not reading the words, though. Not the underlined ones nor any others. I just can't think of anything else to do. I just stare at the symbols on the page. And then it dawns on me what a funny circumstance I'm in. Not just the part about being alone in a café halfway across the planet from home, having run out of the fuel of life while staring at a plate of fried liquid unfertilized chicken gametes. But, all the little things that make up daily life. Including that somehow these carefully arranged spots, which are made by some process unknown to me and kept in place on this flat rectangular dead tree stuff by some other unknown means, are supposed to impart a kind of meaningful message that we've all agreed upon.

And then something unexpected happens. I laugh. Right out loud. And just like in grade school, I can't seem to stop laughing. I try to hold it in, but it keeps bursting out. And so the others in the cafe don't think I'm bat-shit crazy, I pretend it is the book. And I keep on snickering, until eventually I pay the check and leave.

Wandering the streets again, the numbness has taken on a playful hue. The world is colored blue, but it is a blue that is mutable, playing hide-and-seek with other colors, chasing its shadow, feeding the birds, singing to itself. Barefoot, lungi dragging along the dirt streets, no shoulder bag, nowhere to be, no thoughts of when. For now, I have surrendered.

LE PAPE

Number five in the major arcana is called *Le Pape*, the Pope. He wears the uraeus as a crown and carries a triple scepter in his left hand. His right hand is raised, with two fingers pointing up and two fingers pointing down. His throne sits between two pillars. There are two figures kneeling before him, one dark, the other light. A pair of keys are crossed on the ground in front of his feet.

There are two paths for anyone who is seeking to learn that which is kept hidden. One is to initiate into a society, secret or not, with traditions that are well-established. The other is to seek one's own path and to forge the way by trial and error. Either choice is dangerous. In order to master the mysteries of the universe, one must bridge heaven and earth. The bridge is a world in itself.

–THE BOOK OF MYSTERIES

SCYLLA

He sits in the sun-kissed valley. On the other side of the bridge. On the other side of the great falls. On the other side of time.

The water behind him keeps perfect rhythm. It is in synch with the secret heart of hearts. The place where he is can hardly be called a place. For it is not. It is an intersection of worlds. It is a realm unto its own.

It cannot be found on a map. As many courageous souls have learned at their peril. And yet it is not make believe. It is a dream within a dream.

A dream is not what it seems. A dream cannot be bottled and sold. You cannot stake out the boundaries of a dream. You cannot record its title in your name. No photos can be taken of the dream world. And yet it is real.

More real than this page.

PRAEDA

You are at the outdoor spiritual gift-swap again. Or maybe you never left. Anyway, you are sitting cross-legged on red and gold brocade pillows and smoking a hooka with a gaunt Indian man who is wrapped in café au lait colored linen. On his head is a turban made of the same material, accented with sapphires. Gray stubble covers his chin and his face is dry and lined with wrinkles. But his eyes sparkle.

He tells you he knows you from somewhere else. In this other place you keep camels. And occasionally he buys one from you. He calls it the *past now*. He calls you Ramadan. He is a time traveler of sorts. As you sit together on these pillows and share the pipe, he draws in the smoke, and the smoke takes him to other places, other times. Until he has to breathe out.

And then, while you smoke, he exhales and records his journey on a small sketchpad in his lap. He scribbles in a language you don't understand and then he draws pictures to illustrate. You don't think he draws the pictures for you, but you can't be sure.

Is that like a dream journal? You ask.

He nods. *But these things really happen.* He explains.

Dreams really happen. You say.

He stares at you intently for a long moment and you think maybe you have offended him. You also start to become concerned that he is crawling around in your mind without permission. Then he nods ever so slightly, rises, and motions for you to trade places with him. He sits down in your seat and you in his. He gestures and you take up his hose. He shifts the coals on the top and as you begin to inhale, you close your eyes. No sooner are they closed than you are sitting at a table, under a large canvas, across from a younger version of this same man. He is pouring tea into your cup. But you take in too much smoke and cough, opening your eyes and finding yourself back on the red and gold pillows. He laughs heartily and his eyes shine more brightly.

As soon as you catch your breath, he holds up the hose once more and gestures with his head. He explains, *Take a deep breath first and let go. Next take in the smoke from the kea and hold it. Then close your eyes.*

You do as instructed. When you close your eyes, you are back under the large canvas, and he is speaking a language you don't know, but understand. He is telling you the price you've named for the camel, which is hobbled near the tea stand, is not appropriate for an old friend. You nod politely. You remind him that the camel is a young female and can produce other camels for him to use or sell for years to come. You pour more tea for him and motion for another pot. Then you run out of air and have to exhale.

When you wake up, you are no longer on the red and gold pillows, no longer holding the pipe. Instead, you are pouring tea for the otherworldly woman with red hair. You sit on velvet couches, facing one another, in the center of a tiny glade, surrounded by a verdant forest. She appears more goddess than human, more a vision from antiquity, a mythological figure, an archetype.

Let me explain, she begins.

CHARYBDIS

BEFORE I SET OUT ON THIS ADVENTURE, several people told me
of a holy man who lives in the middle of nowhere in Southern
India. He is reported to levitate, to be able to walk several inches
above the ground, to materialize rings and other items out of thin
air, and to produce a sacred ash known as *vibhuti* from his fingers
and his bare feet. He claims to have been born of immaculate
conception, and there are legends that the guru has fed the
multitudes, healed the sick, and raised the dead.

Though his followers have grown to number tens of thousands,
his early audience included George Harrison and John and Yoko.
Citing the necessity of faith, the guru has never submitted to
an examination of his powers under a controlled environment.
At least one inspection of the vibhuti produced from his hands
revealed the source to be incense and cow dung. This last thing
I don't know when I set out for Puttaparthi to find him. I just
think, since it hasn't been a girl, or the hash on the beach, or the
priests at the ghats, or anything else on this journey, maybe he's
the thing I came here to find.

The bus from Hampi to Puttaparthi does not take a direct,
non-stop route. And, like most other public transport in India,
comfort appears never to have been a consideration in its design.
I arrive in town just after 10 pm, tired and dirty and just wanting
a place to lie down and sleep. I find the gates to the ashram easily

enough, but I am turned away, along with two other pilgrims. Turns out, the compound closes at 10 pm and there are no exceptions. We are advised that admissions begin again at 7 am.

The streets are dark and the town—what else there is of it—is also closed up. Not even a food stall to turn to. Somewhat experienced by now in navigating these surprises, I manage to find a cheap room where I can try to recover from my journey with a night's sleep. At least that is the plan. But the mosquitoes have another one. I'm safely tucked inside a mosquito net, which is capable of protecting my skin. But the mosquitoes have a back-up plan. Armed with their tiny, metallic audio-assault weapons, they swarm my would-be resting place with inhuman tenacity. This goes on until I am simply too tired to care and pass out from exhaustion.

The light from the outside world finds its way in to my room sooner than I'd like. I splash my face and brush my teeth with bottled water. Then I fasten up my backpack and head back to the compound. I stop for chai at a stall near the gates and wait for the official unlocking, which doesn't actually happen at 7, as advertised.

The scene on the inside is a little hard to describe without sounding like I'm making it up. But I swear I'm on the set of another remake of Stepford Wives. Everywhere there are Westerners walking around in white robes with a zombie-like bliss on their faces. I keep telling myself to keep an open mind. Because really, what do I know about enlightenment?

Inside the ashram's office, I discover I'll have to surrender my passport in order to check in. I am not happy about this. Most backpackers I've met would not be happy about this. A passport is the traveler's equivalent of a Linus blanket. Usually you just show the passport and let the owner write down the information.

Giving it up feels a little like handing over my plane ticket home to a random stranger. But ok, I'm here to step out of my comfort zone. I can surrender this much.

Then comes the next hit: I can't rent a room, because there's only one of me. The rooms are all two-person rooms. They won't even let me pay double. The penance for being single? I have to sleep in the equivalent of a parking space on a concrete floor in a big warehouse.

But wait, there's more. The helper who shows me to my parking space explains that we need to go get my mattress. I'm assuming they keep them in a different building and check them out to guests as needed. So, he explains, I'll need to leave my backpack (unlocked, unattended) in my designated parking space, while we walk over to god-knows-where and fetch said mattress. Ok, another surrender.

As we walk back across the winding compound, I wonder where exactly we are going. Then we approach the gate again... and keep going. Finally I ask my Puttaparthi bellhop where exactly the mattresses are kept. He points across the street to a small shop where mattresses are stacked up for sale. Yep, that's not a misprint, for *sale*. I explain that I'm only here a couple of days, do they buy it back when I leave? *No*. But I can leave it at the ashram (where they will no doubt collect it and resell it at least several hundred more times). When I bristle—this goes way beyond surrender—my helper tells me I can buy a grass mat, if I like, instead. Ok, at least I can take that with me. So I buy a mat, for about what a grass mat would cost in the States.

On my way back to my parking space, I approach a pavilion where the 8 am session with his holiness is about to begin. I already have a mat. So I take off my sandals and leave them by the wall outside the platform, with a hundred other pairs of shoes.

Turns out, the white-clad people floating around the compound have nothing on the chanting supplicants who make up the greatest portion of the audience this morning. I keep repeating the mantras of openness and acceptance, despite the numerous surprises and disappointments of the last 12 hours. Ultimately though, it doesn't help.

To cut to the chase, Baba does not walk on air, nor does he produce any vibhuti from his fingertips, nor make any rings or other gifts appear from thin air. There are no miracle cures, no one gets up and walks away from a wheelchair, and the masses are not fed from two fish and five loaves of bread. After church is over, I wait for the crowd to thin a little before I roll up my mat and walk down the stairs to where I left my footwear. I find sandals, but instead of my comfortable Tevas, in their place I find a pair of blown-out flip-flops.

Gone is the surrender mantra. I search frantically among the few remaining pairs of footwear before it becomes painfully clear that someone has stolen my shoes. Not mistaken one pair of Tevas for another, but simply stolen them. It is here I completely lose it, start cursing out loud, and sprint barefoot back to my parking space, where at least my backpack still awaits. Seemingly intact.

I unzip it and dig out my running shoes. At least no one has stolen them. I pull them on, strap on my backpack, and march back to the office where I am now convinced I foolishly left my passport. I demand they give it back to me, immediately. When they hesitate, I walk over to the stacks of passports on a long table and, before anyone can stop me, I pick up one stack after another and flip though them until I find mine. I hold it up in the air to show them and then exit before anyone has time to do anything about it. I pass the armed guards, go through the winding compound, out the front gates, across the street and down to the bus station, where I promptly book the next bus to Bangalore.

Then I go find the nearest cafe and eat some breakfast. While I'm soothing my latest misfortune with chai and masala eggs, I realize there is Western music playing in the background. It is Sting, and the synchronicity of his lyrics comforts me: *Men go crazy in congregations, they only get better one by one. One by one.*

LE JUDGMENT

THE TWENTIETH NUMBERED MAJOR ARCANA is called *Le Judgment*. The Archangel Gabriel blows a trumpet while looking out from the sky over a number of men, women, and children who appear to be rising from graves. The angel holds a white banner with a red cross. In the background are blue and white mountains, resembling tidal waves on the ocean.

All journeys meet crossroads. Where the river ends, the ocean begins. We must have the courage to embark on these journeys, to choose our paths, and to let go of the boat once we are across the river.

–THE BOOK OF MYSTERIES

SCYLLA

ONCE OVER THE BRIDGE, the world he encounters is beyond comprehension. He does not possess the vision of Master Rinpoche. Nor the skills of other masters. He followed his own path here. Many times he had to just be still and wait. *When in doubt,* teach the masters, *be still. When certain, be still.*

He has rested, without closing his eyes, without lying down, for what could be many days. It is impossible to know. He is not aware of days and nights here. There is no separation of the worlds.

Even though he searched in darkness, he can see now that on his long journey, his dance has not gone unnoticed. It has been answered over and over by the Song of Songs. The Song has many voices, some of them unspoken, but not unseen. The Song appears as messages on the faces of leaves, the mighty trunks of trees, and the sheer walls of rock. The stones speak the Song to him in an alphabet of colors and in the visible histories of landscapes. The birds mark paths only they can see from their high views. The leaves mark time with the seasons and the weather. The wind uses the trees to tell its tales. And the messages of water are translated for him by the Dorje.

These things are all part of him, as he is part of them, as asleep and awake are two points on the same circle. *It is impossible to fall out of harmony with creation. It is only possible to forget how to see.*

He can see clearly all this and more.

PRAEDA

You awake at a table under a canvas tent on a dusty street. The woman with red hair sits across from you, the lions seated on the ground to her right and left. She breaks a piece of unleavened bread in two and hands one half to you. The green of her eyes cuts a fierce path across the table, forces open the shutters around your heart. You sit before her paralyzed and naked, but unwilling to look away.

You know who I am. She says.

Do I? You say, though you know she knows you have some idea. You're just unable to put words to it.

You neither one say anything. The lions shift their weight from one side to the other, then settle back down. They gaze preternaturally at her, at you, at the world around you. She waits. Patient. A breeze blows. The canvas rustles. Steam rises slowly, hypnotically from your cups of tea.

You are empty of words, of thought, of sound, and completely alive. A full sail on a silent ocean. A white light in a clear blue sky. You have lost all sense of motion. There is no past or future, no backwards or forwards about you at all. In this moment, you simply are. You both are. There is not a word for it.

What she means is this:

I am the thing. I am the beloved. I am your heart of hearts.

What happens after you find the thing you've been searching for?

CHARYBDIS

I HAVE ESCAPED FROM PUTTAPARTHI TO BANGALORE. I find a place that is short on charm and has a small mosquito problem, but I'm getting used to that. The room is also spacious and has geckos scaling the walls. So I figure that's good luck.

Bangalore is really two cities in one, old and new. At first, I explore them both in equal measure. I wander the streets in the old town during the day, getting lost in the alleys, and tucking in with locals at the small chai stalls. At night, I hang out in the new part of town, in a bar called Top Gun. (The entrance is made to look like the mouth of a jet.) The bar is as ridiculous as it sounds, but it has good beer, and it's a place I can stretch out at a table and read or write in my journal. I am insulated, but still out in the world, still enmeshed in the energetic hum of other humans.

I go to see a Hindi blockbuster movie. Well done, but the same basic script as most Hindi films. There is always a crisis to be overcome, like all good storytelling, a transformation which needs to occur. In this case, love needs to find the light of day and blossom despite the dark clouds of the caste system. I don't want to spoil it, but on script with the formula, there is happy dancing and singing near the end.

I meet a guy at Top Gun who is studying Sanskrit at a nearby monastery. He's a white guy who was born in Mexico. I guess that's how he justifies calling me a Gringo. He's a little nuts—I guess you'd have to be to do what he is doing—but he's good for interesting conversation. He says he wants to read the ancient texts, in order to have an authentic interpretation of their meaning and not what someone else tells him they say. I can respect this. Though for as open-minded as this sounds, he is pretty dogmatic in his views. Because, really, whatever the ancient words are, just because something is written down doesn't mean it's true. Ultimately, his dogma proves the undoing of our short friendship.

I soon tire of the new part of town and the ludicrous bar. I'm thinking about my dreams more and more. Wondering what the stories they tell me could mean. Wondering what is real and not real. I sit in my room, in food stalls, even sometimes on the curb, with my feet in the street, and write down as many thoughts as I can. I go back to the beginning of my journal and re-read the notes from my travels so far. I keep thinking I must have missed something. Like when you know you've had a watershed dream, but you just can't quite remember the details. Maybe I did something, met someone, had a single epiphany that I recorded, but forgot. Because, really, this can't be all there is.

I wander the old town more and more. I feel more at home in its dirty streets, among the crumbling buildings, where the cows roam free, where the animals recycle the waste, where the beggars are humble, where men stand on the street in front of chai stalls, talking and drinking their chai from saucers. Where I won't be judged for looking wide-eyed, crooked-smiled, and lost. Where I can empty myself.

LE MONDE

THE NUMBER TWENTY-ONE in the major arcana is called *Le Monde*, the World. A dancing, naked woman wears only a thin scarf, wrapped over her shoulder and around her waist. She holds a wand in each hand, and—like the Hanged Man—her legs are crossed to form the alchemical symbol of Sulphur.

In the four corners are Cherubim, each with a different face—human, lion, ox, and eagle—indicating the four elements. The naked woman is the fifth element. She celebrates completeness, the end of a long journey, and finding one's place in the world. The stars in the wreath that surrounds her reflect her enlightenment. The falling scarf is the unveiling of her truth.

–THE BOOK OF MYSTERIES

SCYLLA

THE DORJE AND THE LAND ARE ONE. They cannot be separated into this and that, over here is the river and over there the land. All things bleed together.

The desert still has a memory of water. And that memory is a living thing. It is infused into the sand. It is part of its essence.

He is also in the land. And the land is in him. As the river is in his blood, the wind his breath. The great birds are his aspirations, his longer vision, his higher self. Just as he is their grounding, their refuge, their sense of place. Each person, each thing, each beast, each thought, each breath, each leaf, each ray of sun, each drop of rain, each bend of light, are all life's metaphors, all refractions from the one prism. This is the poem of life.

The key is to come to rest in the universe's pulse. To release oneself to its care, its rhythm, its sway. This letting go is called many things. The act of letting go is the act of loving. It is falling into love. And love is the highest act possible.

All things dance the same dance, in and out of step, in perfect harmony with the rhythm of the universe, which is not linear, not predictable. Sometimes it strides, others it loafs. The universe wanders. Its journey is everything's journey.

He has fallen into its rhythm. He has found his way.

PRAEDA

MANY YEARS AFTER ASHOKA'S REIGN, the world finds itself at a new crossroads. A new bridge to be crossed. A new moon coming. And a new white lion being born, once again into the land known as Timbavati.

The world and its leaders have become lost once more. And so the lion Aragon roams in search of a new messenger. One who can walk in this new world and bring to it his ancient wisdom. Over vast distances the lion calls. Dropping hints, scattering synchronicities, and appearing in dreams. Until a plan is set in motion.

After a long and difficult journey, the new messenger makes it to his destination in the protected forest. Though he believes he is still lost. The messenger searches the forest by morning, looking for something unknown, looking for an avatar to guide him to where he needs to go. He wanders the food stalls by night, talking to locals and listening to stories of lion encounters.

Aragon knows he cannot just approach this one the way the legendary beasts did in ages past. He'll have to be more clever. He drops clues in his path, staying close enough to keep the messenger looking. Close enough to whisper into his ear. *If you stop looking so hard, you'll find what you need. You only need to stop and listen. The story is all around you.*

And though he hears, the messenger does not stop. Not right away, anyway. His restlessness gets the best of him and he boards a train for the South. On the train, resting his head on his backpack, his belly filled with masala dosa, he hears the voice again. *Stop and listen. The story is everywhere.*

CHARYBDIS

EVERYONE KEEPS SAYING YOU CAN GET a good glass of wine in Pondicherry, because it used to be a French colony. Wanting something besides chai and beer and to experience both the Arabian Sea and the Bay of Bengal, I decide to come here. I stay at the Aurobindo Ashram, not because I'm looking for spiritual guidance there, but because it is inexpensive and quiet.

I spend more time walking than I have lately. In truth, that is mostly what I do. I walk. I walk so much that I wake up with stiff and sore legs. I walk along the rock wall of the long Promenade, splashed by water from the Bay. I walk along the rim of the city, and from cafe to cafe. I walk through all the different sectors of the town, the French Quarter, the Muslim Quarter, the Hindu Quarter, and the Christian Quarter, and then back along the oceanfront. I walk, therefore I am.

*   *   *   *

I arrive back at the ashram after another full day of walking. At some point in my wandering I must have fallen into a trance-like state. When I left, the only thing in my pocket was my room key. Coming back at the end of the day, I reach into my pocket and discover that the key is sharing space with a number of other objects. In my fatigue, I can't quite make sense of this. Once inside,

I slip off my shoes and empty the contents of my pocket onto the nightstand. Apparently, in my trance, I was collecting small treasures from around the city. The largest is a dark gray piece of clay, with a faint streak of white showing on one side. My mind is too tired to sort out the riddle, and I climb straight into bed with my clothes on and fall fast asleep, the piece of clay still in my hand.

*   *   *   *

In my dream, I am standing at a workbench in a space lit by candles. The workbench is cluttered with containers of liquids, stones, flints, and stacks of rough-edged papers smeared with ink and ash. My fingers are stained. There is a measuring device on the table I don't recognize.

I cannot see what it is my hands are working with, only that occasionally there is a flash of white light and then a show of colors.

*   *   *   *

When I awake, there is something egg-shaped, smooth, and hard in my hand. I open up my fingers and resting in my palm is a stone that is pitch black in color and has a white spot on one side. The stone has an alluring feel to it, almost as if it is vibrating, but on a frequency too high to measure. The spot gives the illusion of a miniature painting of gathering clouds, or a cluster of a billion tiny stars shining out from the stone's dark night, like it has its own Milky Way.

LE CHARIOT

THE NUMBER SEVEN IN THE MAJOR ARCANA is called *Le Chariot*, the Chariot. A victorious charioteer rides a winged chariot drawn by two sphinxes, one black and one white. Waxing and waning moons sit on either shoulder of the charioteer. He carries a magician's wand and wears a tunic adorned with alchemical symbols. The chariot is covered by a canopy of stars held up by four pillars.

The long journey of life reveals a union of opposites. Things are not always what they seem. Our friends may become enemies and our enemies, friends. The hero of any journey must travel over water and land, through the conscious and unconscious, must bridge heaven and earth, and answer the riddle of the sphinx. All bearers of the light will eventually find transformation.

—THE BOOK OF MYSTERIES

SCYLLA

HE AWAKES FROM A DREAM he has had several times. In the dream, he is a young man on a long journey, far from home. He is not dressed in his traditional robes, but much differently, in a manner he has only seen in visions.

*   *   *   *

In the dream, he is near despair. He is looking for an answer to a question he has not yet asked. While he travels, he meets many people, each of whom has wisdom to share. But because he is looking for a grand treasure, he cannot see the small gifts he finds along the way. He does not yet understand the reflective nature of the universe. And so he cannot see that the grand treasure lies dormant in his own heart.

*   *   *   *

The monk now understands the reason for this continuing dream. The young man has come to him for a kind of refuge, which only he is able to provide. He resolves to give him three things. He will teach him the secret of the three worlds. He will watch over his journey and help keep him on his path. And finally, he will share with him the stone gift, the one from his master, so that the young man might work his own alchemy. So that he might complete the transubstantiation of his own heart.

PRAEDA

YOU AWAKE ON THE SMALL CARPET, overlooking the lush, green cliffs. And she is there with you once again. Sitting on a pillow directly across from yours, her red hair framing her graceful features, her white linen falling softly from her shoulders. She looks at you tenderly, but with an otherworldly assuredness. *You want to know more about what I said before. More about why you've been following me. Why we're here.*

You don't know how to respond. You don't know how to even begin to respond. So you just say the first thing that falls out of your mouth. *I think I'm following you because I'm completely lost, and I have no idea where to go next. All of life seems to be just tilting at windmills.*

She sits peacefully in front of you, calm and composed. Then she reaches out her hands, palms open, relaxed. You extend yours to meet hers. And the instant you touch her hands, you are pulled into her world. A beautiful, clear, and infinite world, where you feel no line between the two of you. Where you can hear her thoughts without effort.

It is simple. Everything must break open in order to live. The seed must break open in order for the tree to grow. The egg must break open in order for life to emerge. The Earth must be turned and the cloud must burst. You were never meant to stay in your shell.

Do not run away from pain. And do not be aloof to joy. Embrace it all. As the teaching says, live like a mighty river. Stop trying to hold all the beauty you encounter, to keep it safe inside you. Embrace your frailties, embrace your inability to hold it all. Just let it spill out. That's where it belongs, out, in the open. Free.

A good life is not free of messiness. A good life is a full one. Full of beauty and ugliness, comfort and pain, loneliness and belonging. So be unconditional. Be fearless in your willingness to live all of it. The sacred land you seek is within you. Everything in the world, all of it, is already inside you. But you can't really see it until you open the door and let it roam free.

CHARYBDIS

I AM IN CHENNAI, still on the Bay of Bengal. I'm not sure why I left Pondicherry, except I just couldn't stay at the ashram anymore. Maybe it's a good thing the green-eyed beauty took my money, forcing me home early, because I think I'm over India. I haven't found what I was looking for here. I'm tired of the kind of attention my light skin and blue eyes attract, tired of people yelling and clamoring for me to give them money or to buy something I don't need. I'm tired of not having any personal space.

I don't mean to be ungrateful. It isn't that India hasn't been wild, wonderful, and filled with beautiful discoveries. But maybe I've just had too much. Maybe I need some time to process all this, to make sense of why I came here and what any of these experiences mean. Or maybe there's been too much time to think. Maybe I need to go back home and lose myself doing anything besides thinking.

I still eat in local food stalls and search for out-of-the-way places to have a cup of chai. During the day, I still wrap myself in a shawl and attempt to blend into the backstreets. To have quiet conversations with local men over steaming hot saucers of tea. But at night, I make my way to the Taj Hotel and I sit down at a table with a tablecloth. I listen to live piano music and eat a nice dinner. I read a book, listen to the music, and take my time.

I hardly look like a proper guest at the Taj, wearing worn linen and cheap Indian sandals. My room, like so many others I've had in India, is nothing to write about. It is a simple concrete walk-up. It costs almost nothing, so I'm able to spend what money I have left on these dinners at the Taj.

Tonight, in a fit of desperation for the entertainment equivalent of comfort food, I go to see a James Bond movie, simply because it's in English. This turns out to be a stroke of genius. It is like taking a bubble bath after running a marathon. I had no idea I could like James Bond so much. I stay in the theatre until the last credit has rolled. Slowly I get up and make my way out of the theatre to the still-bustling Indian street.

I decide to take a different way back to my room, for the sake of adventure, but also to stay out of sight as much as possible. On the way, I see a small sign for a psychic, it reads: *Fortune Telling, Palm Reading, Dream Interpretation*. I pass by the door at first, then turn around, walk up the steps, and ring the bell. I wait, but nothing happens. I ring again. And a third time. Finally I try the door. It is open, so I walk in. I go through a couple of layers of hanging fabric before I make my way into the main chamber.

I am greeted by a woman in traditional Indian clothing who is sitting behind a counter of sorts. She looks up from some activity I can't see. And I am immediately taken by her eyes. They shine in the dimly lit room as if they were backlit.

Hello. She says, simply.

Hello. I finally say in return.

May I help you? She offers.

I rang the bell... Is all I can manage.

Oh, that hasn't worked for years. She explains.

Oh. Is all I say.

Is that what you wanted to talk about? The doorbell? She asks, politely.

Well, no. I hesitate. *You can tell people about their dreams?*
Sometimes.

How do I know if this is one of those times?

Well, I suppose you won't. She explains. *In my experience, life rarely comes with guarantees.*

Ok. I say as I look around the room. *How do we start?*

Come with me.

I follow her through another layer of hanging fabric and into a room with only pillows on the floor. She gestures and I sit. She reaches out her hands to me and I lift mine to meet them. She closes her eyes and sits still for a moment. I think about closing mine, but I'm too curious, so I leave them open. I watch her eyelids, looking for some sign of what is going on behind them. I get nothing. Slowly she opens her eyes again.

You have a particular dream you want to share with me?

Yes, I do. I begin.

I have this dream that I am in India. I am on a quest of some kind. I'm traveling around, meeting interesting people, climbing hills, kneeing in sacred places, walking barefoot through the Taj Mahal, getting overcharged by rickshaw drivers, getting harassed by baksheesh beggars, drinking cold beer on white-sand beaches, renting scooters, exploring ancient ruins, reading books, collecting email addresses, wearing lungis, learning to chew paan, scribbling in my journal, eating bhang chocolate, dancing with strangers, going three weeks without shoes, taking impossibly long train rides, eating with my fingers, chasing holy men, washing in Ghats, taking blurry photos, drinking cup after cup of chai, sharing rooms with strangers and with all manner of crawling things, falling in love, getting my heart smashed, getting robbed, and somehow continuing on, to the next train, the next city, the next cup of chai. I pause. *What do you think this means?*

She waits for several moments, sitting still, calm, hands in her lap. Then she begins.

There are three worlds in which we live. There is the waking world. There is the spirit world. And there is the dream world, the bridge between the other two. The secrets of the spirit world are brought to the waking world over the dream world's bridge. But the act of carrying this information over the bridge is not an easy one.

Many ancient and modern texts have been written about the spirit world. Many stories are told about life in the waking world. About the dream world, though, little is known. It is the least understood and perhaps the most important to the human experience.

The story you just told me is the dream of your waking life. Until you can see clearly, the universe presents all things to you in the form of dreams.

It is important for you, I think, to understand that you are everything in your dreams. You are the monsters you run from. You are the women you make love to. You are the buildings and the houses and the furniture. You are the fears and the joys, the treasures and the pain. You are the labyrinths. You are the disappointment and the relief that you wake up to.

When you can unlock your dream life, your waking life will follow. Because everything in your waking life is also a metaphor, a reflection, a refraction of something bigger. Just like in your dream world. You are this room. You are the words I am speaking. Then she pauses, and making sure I am under the trance of her eyes, she continues. *You are the lions of India. You are all the metals of the Earth, spun into gold. You are Vishnu, dreaming the world into being.*

When she stops talking, she reaches behind her and produces a small hookah pipe with two hoses. She places the pipe between us and lights two coals for the top. Afterwards, she reaches up and removes two hairpins. Slowly she unwraps the scarf from around her head and lays it in folds on a pillow next to her. Then she reaches up again and removes more pins. In the dim light of the room, as her hair begins to come down, I recognize its color.

She picks up the hoses from the hookah and offers me one.

Join me? She says.

LE SOLEIL

NUMBER NINETEEN IN THE MAJOR ARCANA is called *Le Soleil*, the Sun. A naked, laughing child plays in a garden surrounded by sunflowers. The child rides upon a white horse without the assistance of a saddle or reins, carrying only a red banner. The sun has risen above the wall of the garden, shining twenty-one curvy and straight rays of light.

Each day begins with renewed innocence and purity. Dawn always follows the dark night. The rising sun illuminates simple beauty. It reminds us of the marriage of light and dark, of the unity of all things.

–THE BOOK OF MYSTERIES

SCYLLA

It is time to make his way back to his village. He knows the way now and so the journey home is easier. The terrain of the sacred mountain is familiar to him, as he is familiar to it. He knows the Dorje will not lead him astray.

His journey has transformed him. He is lighter.

He has no need for the heavy pack any longer. The Dorje feeds him when he is hungry. The rock ledges shelter him when it rains. The deep forest floor invites him to rest. He follows the river through the valleys. He follows the mountain goats across the steep cliffs. The full moon leads him through the darkness.

The dawn approaches. The songbirds celebrate. He has opened his eyes.

PRAEDA

AFTER THE FLEETING BEAUTY OF DAWN will come a new sun. Like the pure white of the sun, the full spectrum of light will arise again under the subtle force of the alchemist's hands. This second coming will be more complete, more sure of itself. You will drape the subject of your art in a flowing robe of white, protecting it, shrouding it, and then, at last, slowly revealing its secret heart.

This is the penultimate test, the final purification. In order to hold this space, you must imagine the sacred unicorn bending to the rose's beauty, the pure white pelican feeding its young, Snow White and the blood-red apple.

As the crimson secret heart is revealed, so the center of the alchemist's soul is transformed. Only when your soul has made this opening, this ascendance, this transmutation, will rebirth be possible.

Only when you are able to bring together all the colors of the mandala, to make a circle of the snake, to seduce the dragon with its own tail, will the illusions of the dual world be revealed. Only then will you see clearly that you are whole. And only a whole person, only a fully realized being, only an artist who has the courage to find his secret heart and to reveal it to the world, can call himself a master, an alchemist.

Only an alchemist can forge the key that opens the door to the heart's secret chamber, that place in every human chest where the golden beauty of the universe lies waiting to be released. Every human heart longs for the release of its own phoenix, to burn and burn and burn in golden splendor.

The gold itself is nothing, the transformation everything.

CHARYBDIS

I am in Varanasi, a long way from Chennai. I'm not sure why I'm here, except it called to me, and it didn't care that I was tired and almost out of money. It took me more than two days on trains to get here. Mostly, I slept. I didn't think a person could sleep for the better part of 48 hours, not unless he was in a coma. But I pretty much did. I woke up twice to eat. And I had to change trains once. But even then I slept in the station while waiting. Luckily, another backpacker woke me up in time to catch my train. After three months in India, he was headed for the airport to go home. As I was boarding, he handed me a rumpled envelope and said, *I don't need what's in here. But I think you might. Have fun on the rest of your journey.* Then he bowed a *Namaste* and I returned the gesture. He took off before I could say anything or even look at the contents of the envelope. Inside the train, I made my way to the restroom to examine the gift away from curious eyes. Looking back at me was a thick stack of colorful rupees, variously rumpled and crisp, mostly with the numbers 100 and 500 in their corners. At a glance, easily enough for a backpacker to live on for a month or two.

Varanasi is the most spectacular place I've ever seen. It is a dense city, packed with buildings and people and layers upon layers of history. It is old, really old. No one actually knows exactly how old. People have lived here since at least the 11th century

B.C.E., maybe before. Take everything else I've seen in India, every place I've been, everyone I've met, everything I've learned and experienced, stack it all together, and Varanasi still beats it. Nothing I could say could convey to you what it's like to be here, though. There is a reason Indians everywhere refer to it as the spiritual capital of India. Not that it needs a slogan. It speaks for itself.

There are places in the world that have a different vibration. I don't know if it is higher, or stronger, or maybe louder, I just know it feels different to be in those places. This is one of those places, and I feel more awake here, more at home. Varanasi calls out to its pilgrims, just as it did to me. I was far away from this city. I was ready to leave India. I was out of money, headed to Bangkok, then back to the States. But Varanasi would not let me leave. Without reason or logic, I found myself at the train station, backpack in tow, buying the next and cheapest rail passage here. As soon as I stepped off the train I knew why. This is not the grandeur of Vienna, not the bohemian rhythm of Prague, not the relaxed beauty of Benaulim, it is all of these and more.

Death is celebrated more than life in Varanasi. A pilgrimage to Varanasi, to bathe in the holy river Ganges, is considered essential to Hindus at some time during their lives. To die in Varanasi is considered auspicious. To have your body burned on the pyres beside the river and your remains scattered on the Ganges releases your soul from the burden of rebirth. The pyres burn almost constantly. Every day the smoke from the cremation ghats is thick throughout the city. And yet I can breathe better here than any place I've been in India. Death is everywhere, and yet I've never felt more alive.

I wake up every morning before the sun, tie on my lungi, and walk down the dusty streets to the nearest bathing ghat. I bow to the priest, who is already there tending his duties. He burns incense, places fresh flower petals in a bowl of holy water, strings marigolds, and lays out other offerings for pilgrims. Many colorful boats are tied near the shore. A few are filled with stacks of fresh wood for the ritual fires. Nearby, those tending a cremation ghat are gathering up ashes from the night before and pouring them into the Ganges.

I descend the steps, remove my shoes, and hand the priest a suitable baksheesh, usually a few rupees, but he will also accept incense, drinking water, or charas. I bow and then descend the steps into the murky water. I don't know if it is in my mind, or if the river actually has healing powers. Maybe it is the collective human vibration from centuries of reverence that has been deposited here. Whatever the reason, it is a powerful baptism. And the best morning ritual I can imagine. I feel it as soon as the water touches my toes. And by the time I get to my head, I've slipped the bonds of Earth. Going under the water, I dissolve for a moment into liquid Nirvana.

I make my way back out of the water and sit on the steps to dry. I watch the red sun begin to wake up and stretch itself into the dawn, and then I close my eyes. I stay here until the warmth of the rising sun removes the damp shawl from my shoulders and invites me to morning tea. Like many other places in India, this city is a frenetic dance of colors and lights, sounds and smells, people and animals. There is noise and smoke and baksheesh beggars, chaos and traffic and often little personal space. But there is a lightness to everything here. The people have a gentle manner, smiles on their faces, light in their eyes. Perhaps being this close to death all day, every day, has allowed them to be humble and kind. Whatever the reason, there is a great sense of peace here.

When I leave the ghat, I walk into the old town, where the winding alleyways intentionally try to get me lost. The streets gradually narrow, until no traffic is able to fit through, and people must brush up against one another to pass. Along the way, though, there are cobbled and dusty streets, food and chai stalls, silks and other handmade goods, candle-lit shrines carved into the walls, and thousands of lighted faces. I spend most of my days here, quietly lost in these tangled mazes, bowing and smiling, sharing tea with shop owners.

At night, I go to the evening puja ritual at Dasaswamedh ghat. As if the whole of Varanasi were not enough, the evening puja is an added feast for the senses. There is chanting and music, cymbals and dancing, incense and fires. The ghat is lit up with all manner of lights and flames, including little flower boats carrying tea lights that are floated down the river. I walk down the steps to a woman selling the tiny boats and pay her for one. Then I walk upstream on the ghats for a while, away from the puja ritual, where I wade into the sacred water and release my delicate, lighted boat. I watch as it floats downstream, joining other boats, creating a lighted caravan of colors. I watch until the light of my little boat merges with those of the other boats and with the reflections of the ritual fires, all the lights becoming one. Then I climb back out of the water and sit on the steps of the ghat, entranced by the rhythms of the ritual, seduced by its sights, intoxicated by its smells.

Tomorrow, I will do it all again.

PRAEDA

You are at the outdoor market, sitting on a simple pillow, on a purple rug, meditating on the beauty all around you, when a feather floats down through the sky and lands in your lap. You look down at it. It is pure white, not a spot of color or dirt anywhere.

After a moment, you reach out a weathered hand to pick up the feather so you may get a closer look. Before you can touch it, though, a breeze lifts the feather gently from your lap and places it in the lap of a young man who is sitting across from you.

The young man is a youthful image of you, his face suntanned and thin. He wears blue linen and is barefoot. He, too, sits cross-legged. His eyes glint and his smile is easy. Even so, you see he has known some hardships on his path.

The young man looks down at the feather. He also reaches out to pick it up, when it lifts from his lap and comes to rest between the two of you.

What do you suppose this means? You ask him.

The young man sits for a moment, considering the feather, a hint of a smile on his face. Then he looks up at you, his eyes shining, and answers. *I have a book on mythology, a gift from a friend. I read in it about the ancient Egyptians and their death rites. According to the hieroglyphs, when you die, you travel to the underworld, where Anubis, who shepherds the souls of the dead, places your heart on one* side of a scale and a feather on the other. *If your heart is as light as the feather, you are free to ascend to the next realm.*

You smile back at him.

And what do you think it means? He asks in return.

You consider your words in silence, putting space between the question and the answer. *I've been thinking about dreams a great deal lately. Like the feather, a dream is hard to catch. But when we become light, like the feather, we are able to float on the wind. Then there is no need to capture our dreams. We become them.*

ACKNOWLEDGMENTS

No matter how independent or solitary one may be, none of us accomplishes anything on our own. This novel is in your hands because of the efforts—big and small—of countless people, and any list of names I could compile would necessarily be incomplete. But there are those who so directly contributed to this work I am moved to put their names in print here. To Leslie M. Browning and everyone at Homebound Publications, thank you for taking me into the fold and treating me like family. To Oliver X, for your unwavering belief in me and this work. To Peter, who will not read this, but who is as solid a friend as one could hope for all the same. To Tracey, who knows me as well as any human, still remains my friend, and helps to keep me sane. To Lorna, for her many gifts of the heart. To Lynell, who daily helps me do the hardest job in the world (parenting) and who also makes sure we still have regular date nights. And to August, you remain my greatest teacher.

Finally, to all the faithful readers who have reached out to me over the years to tell me I have made a difference in your days, your words have made all the difference.

ABOUT THE AUTHOR

Thomas Lloyd Qualls is a writer, a condition that is apparently incurable. He lives and writes in the high desert beauty of Northern Nevada, along with the children's author Lynell Garfield and their son August. He is a former copywriter, a licensed attorney who has overturned two death sentences, and a one-time vagabond who regularly wandered the globe with a backpack and three changes of clothes.

Thomas is also the co-creator of several video storytelling projects and the former owner of a music festival, as well as a sometimes painter and a contributor of words to *Rebelle Society*, *Wild Heart Writers*, and *Reno Tahoe Tonight Magazine*.

With all these projects, he seeks to build bridges between people and to foster positive curiosity about each other and this beautiful crazy world.

You can follow his trail of words and his other misadventures at www.tlqonline.com.

HOMEBOUND PUBLICATIONS

Ensuring that the mainstream isn't the only stream.

AT HOMEBOUND PUBLICATIONS, we publish books written by independent voices for independent minds. Our books focus on a return to simplicity and balance, connection to the earth and each other, and the search for meaning and authenticity. We strive to ensure that the mainstream is not the only stream. In all our titles, our intention is to introduce new perspectives that will directly aid humankind in the trials we face at present as a global village.

WWW.HOMEBOUNDPUBLICATIONS.COM
LOOK FOR OUR TITLES WHEREVER BOOKS ARE SOLD

SINCE 2011